THE AFFLICTION

Also by C. Dale Young

The Halo
Torn
The Second Person
The Day Underneath the Day

THE AFFLICTION

A NOVEL IN STORIES

C. DALE YOUNG

Four Way Books
Tribeca

Library of Congress Cataloging-in-Publication Data

Names: Young, C. Dale, author.
Title: The affliction : a novel in stories / C. Dale Young.
Other titles: Short stories. Selections
Description: Tribeca : Four Way Books, [2018]
Identifiers: LCCN 2017029361 (print) | LCCN 2017031107 (ebook) | ISBN
9781945588167 (ebook) | ISBN 9781945588068 (softcover : acid-free paper)
Classification: LCC PS3625.O96 (ebook) | LCC PS3625.O96 A6 2018 (print) | DDC
813/.6--dc23
LC record available at https://lccn.loc.gov/2017029361

This book is manufactured in the United States of America and printed on acid-free paper.

Four Way Books is a not-for-profit literary press. We are grateful for the assistance
we receive from individual donors, public arts agencies, and private foundations.

PROUD MEMBER

[clmp]

We are a proud member of the Community of Literary Magazines and Presses.

Distributed by University Press of New England
One Court Street, Lebanon, NH 03766

for my family

CONTENTS

One doesn't die when he should, but when he can.

—Gabriel García Márquez
One Hundred Years of Solitude

I. The Affliction

No one would have believed Ricardo Blanco if he had tried to explain that Javier Castillo could disappear. What was the point in trying to explain it to someone, explain how he had seen it himself, how he had watched as Javier Castillo stared deeply as if he were concentrating and then, slowly, disappeared? Ricardo always began the explanation in the same way, by stating that it wasn't a sudden thing, that no, no, it was a gradual thing that took sometimes as long as three minutes.

Ricardo was an odd man, to say the least. He wanted to believe Javier Castillo was a god of some kind. But Ricardo did not believe in gods. He did not even believe in Christmas, angels, or miracles. He barely believed in magic. Ricardo was a man who even found it difficult to believe in kindness. What I can tell you is that Ricardo left his wife and family to follow this man, this Javier Castillo, a man about whom he knew very little at the time. What he learned about Javier Castillo was that he possessed an affliction. This is the very word Javier Castillo apparently used to describe his ability to disappear: "affliction." Ricardo wanted to believe in that, but what he felt was something more like envy. And maybe somewhere within his messed-up head Ricardo believed that the longer he was around Javier Castillo the more likely he, too, would gain this unbelievable ability to disappear.

But Javier Castillo . . . Yes, the really surprising thing about Javier Castillo was not the disappearing act. Anyone can disappear. Even you can disappear. What was remarkable about his ability to disappear was the fact that Javier Castillo had control over where he then reappeared. Imagine that. I cannot be certain when he first demonstrated to Ricardo his "affliction," but I can piece together that it must have been early, sometime within a few days of their first meeting. Did he willingly demonstrate it? Or did Ricardo simply catch him in the act? I'll never really know. What I do know is that Javier Castillo had explained to Ricardo that as a boy he moved from a very small island in the Caribbean to Los Angeles to live with his aunt for a while, from one decaying former realm of Spain to another. He explained how one night, as he lay in bed, he wanted to be back on the island so badly he closed his eyes and tried to imagine being there. He thought, for a moment, that he could actually see the Old Square. And when he opened his eyes, he was lying on a ledge. He was lying on the lip of the Spanish fountain in the center of the Old Square, the fountain cascading over the flowering tree of sculpted concrete down into the shallow pool next to him. He thought the warm and humid night was a dream. He thought he was having a spectacular dream. But he was not dreaming.

Had he been dreaming, the shallow pool would be speckled with the reflections of gold coins dotting the royal blue tile beneath the fountain, and the tiles would be without the cracks and missing pieces that had been a feature of that fountain for so many years. But there were definitely no gold doubloons with the easy-to-recognize cross in their centers, each arm of the cross equal. In a different kind of dream, there would be coins tossed into the fountain with wishes in mind. But there were definitely no coins there. It was no dream. And no one on that island would have thrown money away, even for a wish.

Javier Castillo was there in the Old Square, the old men strolling around smoking and talking slowly, others leaning against walls beside doorframes like awkward flamingos, one leg firmly planted on the ground, the other leg bent at the knee so that the bottom of the shoe was affixed to the wall behind them. In the distance, Javier Castillo could hear the ever-present sound of the waves arriving at the shore, the large harbor unseen but just beyond the stalls of the flea market. He could hear Spanish and English and even the awkward Creole being spoken around him that assured him he was indeed on the island, that he was nowhere else on this earth. And when he sat up, when Javier Castillo sat up, nothing changed. It was not a dream. It was anything but a dream. Javier Castillo sat up, swung his legs down from the lip of the fountain, took a deep breath and stood up. Nothing changed. Nothing so much as shimmered or wavered the way things do in dreams.

Ricardo recounted to me how when he first heard this story he had closed his own eyes trying to imagine another town. But all Ricardo saw when he closed his eyes was the bluish white glow of the light bulb he had been staring at before he closed his eyes. There was the ring or impression of the bulb on the inside of his eyelids, but nothing more. He could see no other place. The round bluish-white mark on the inside of his eyelids was not even perfectly round. It was hazy and indistinct. It seemed to be disappearing. The light bulb was disappearing, but nothing else was. Ricardo had, at that time, never been outside of the Los Angeles area. He had never gone anywhere except to work at the body shop and to work at LAX and, eventually, to the town in the Valley where Javier Castillo had been living. He could not, try as he might, picture any other place at all. He closed his eyes again and tried then to picture the curb at Departures at LAX. He concentrated but found even the image of a place he had seen evening after evening for years difficult to hold still. Like the light bulb, it was hazy and indistinct.

The recollection of the first time Javier Castillo disappeared stayed with Ricardo, haunted him, lingered in his mind the way the wish for gold coins did for the *Conquistadores*. How could it not? He returned to that story over and over. He couldn't help it. He would tell it to me time and time again as if he were an old man who needed to remember, who needed to tell the story to remind himself of his own past. He would tell it as if he were charged with telling it, recounting it, as if his life somehow depended on it. He did so with what could only be called, for lack of better words, a quiet urgency. Ricardo could hear Javier Castillo's voice in his head describing what had happened to him. He replayed the situation over and over of opening one's eyes and seeing not one's bedroom but a town square on an island thousands of miles away. But what struck Ricardo, what intrigued him, the slim needle of the story that pricked him along his arms and chest repeatedly, was not the oddity of what had happened—the disappearance, the reappearance—but the fact Javier Castillo had not been afraid. Ricardo knew that had such a thing happened to him as a young boy, he would have been terrified. Honestly, I would have been terrified as well. Wouldn't you be? I find it hard to imagine someone who would not have been afraid.

Ricardo Blanco did not know many things, but he knew that had this happened to him he would have sat in the Old Square worrying and wondering how he would ever find his way back to his family in Los Angeles. He knew he was not the kind of man that Javier Castillo was, that he was afraid of being alone. And being in another city surrounded by people you didn't know was essentially being alone. Ricardo needed people, and he needed to know things. And, apparently, this was not something Javier Castillo cared about, not even remotely. Even then, thirty plus years after his first disappearance, Javier Castillo had no understanding of his affliction. He could not explain to Ricardo how it happened. He simply knew he could do it. And this knowledge was enough for him. It was, after all, his affliction, and he knew he had no other choice than to live with it.

As a young man, Ricardo married the girl next door, or so he liked to tell people. His parents had him marry, made him marry, the daughter of their best friends. She was beautiful. Rosa was beautiful, but she was not gorgeous. There was no better way of describing her. To describe her inky black hair or the creamy color of her skin would have been pointless. To describe the softness of her voice, its occasional stutters and the speed that anxieties added to it, and compare it to running water was pointless. What was important was that she was a beautiful woman, and he had walked out on her. And it wasn't just Ricardo who thought she was beautiful. I have heard that exact word used by a number of people over the years to describe Rosa Blanco. What I can say is that on some days Ricardo wondered where she was and what she was doing, but he knew exactly what she was doing. She was worrying about him, their sons, worrying about every aspect of her future.

Ricardo was a worrier, too. But he was very different from his wife in that the worry never grew large, remained small enough for him to hide it away, bury it in his gut. At times, he wondered if his sons Pedro and

Carlitos were being good for their mother. But he felt certain they were not being good. They were boys after all, and he knew boys at their age were trouble or about to be trouble. They couldn't help it. It was not as if they chose to cause trouble; they just did. And his wife? She wanted those boys to be good, which in her eyes meant good in school, good at sports, good at something. But they would never be good in school. They would never understand why school was important. They would never be good at most things. They wanted to be old enough to drive a truck, to be able to drive to the edge of town and get high. Ricardo understood this. He had been a boy just like them. He knew what it was like to get stoned and curse the sky because it was getting dark too quickly. He knew what it was like to smoke until the dryness in the desert became the dryness in your throat. He was no Javier Castillo, and neither were his sons. And frankly, neither was I.

Ricardo explained how he had watched Javier Castillo disappear many times. In many ways, he had studied this affliction, timed it. He visited the library once to look through books on physics. He was sure there would be some explanation within one of those books he believed explained everything about the workings of the natural world. As a child, when he had questions, he could always find the answers in books at the library. Sitting in the stacks on the recently installed new carpets, the fumes from them like a tranquilizing gas, the stacks themselves like corrugated walls, he had tried to read those books the way he had done as a child. None of them had any information on this means of travel he had witnessed, or none that he could make out from the photos and diagrams. There were many images of lines and rays and light bending, but nothing that seemed to explain how one disappeared and, minutes later, appeared somewhere else, how one made such a thing happen.

That Javier Castillo could fade away and then find himself in a new place, Ricardo was fairly certain. Javier Castillo had recounted to him how during his late teens he had gone to Singapore, French Polynesia, and even Egypt. He would find pictures of places in books, concentrate on them, concentrate on the major and unchangeable things in the photos, and then "move himself" to one of these very spots. It was then Ricardo really discovered the extent of Javier Castillo's affliction. He could go to other places for a few hours or a few days. He had spent an entire week in Toronto wandering through Chinatown. Ricardo knew this but could not believe it. He wondered if Javier Castillo ever made mistakes, if he ever materialized inside, say, a wall. He wondered about the "navigation system" of it all. What if he made a mistake while traveling in this way? How did he control all of this? The questions inside Ricardo's head were endless but understandable. You know what happened next; know it as surely as anything. The day came when Ricardo felt the overwhelming need to test Javier Castillo. He needed something more than observation of the disappearing act and the stories then recounted to him later. He wanted proof. He needed proof.

And so, one afternoon, an afternoon not unlike many others, Ricardo wrote four numbers on a scrap of paper and left it on the chest of drawers in the bedroom he shared with Javier Castillo. Ricardo was planning ahead. He was convinced the numbers, which he had seen in a dream, were clues to picking the right horse: 3, 7, 19 and 33. And so, he hatched a plan, thought it through with multiple permutations. This was to be a foolproof test of the man named Javier Castillo, a test to prove once and for all how the "affliction" worked. He wrote down the four numbers and then went into the living room to find Javier Castillo. He persuaded him they needed to go to the horse races that afternoon. It was something to do, something to pass the time, something to ease the boredom. Shortly after arriving at the track, after picking up betting sheets and studying odds, after finding their seats, Ricardo told Javier Castillo about the numbers, told him how he had seen them in a dream and had written them down but had forgotten to bring the paper with him, that he needed them and couldn't remember them. He went on and on about the numbers and how he felt certain, quite certain, that they were very important numbers. He played Javier Castillo well. In this, Ricardo, whether he knew it or not then, was an expert.

Javier Castillo sighed and then excused himself. He climbed the steps from the seats in the stands to the main concourse that was bustling with men of all ages, men darting around filled with the excitement of wagers.

He went into the men's room, entered a stall, locked the gray metal swing-ing door covered with crass graffiti scraped into the paint, and disap-peared. When he reappeared in the stall a few minutes later, he went back to Ricardo and sat next to him, without even the slightest flourish. While at the house, Javier Castillo had written the numbers down on the back of his hand with the black sharpie marker left next to the scrap of paper Ricardo had "forgotten," the marker left there intentionally by Ricardo as part of his test. And when Javier Castillo showed Ricardo all four num-bers written down on the back of his hand, Ricardo said nothing. Ricardo didn't even say thank you. Ricardo wondered, instead, why Javier Castillo had written the numbers on the back of his hand instead of simply bring-ing the piece of paper back with him. Surely this meant something about the affliction. Surely a clue was to be found in this action, the paper still on the chest of drawers but the numbers retrieved and inscribed upon the back of Javier Castillo's hand.

Ricardo never knew what to say to Javier Castillo. Can you blame him? I wouldn't have known back then what to say to a man who could disappear, could travel around the world like air itself. But in Ricardo's case, it wasn't that he couldn't find the words. It was just that Ricardo never felt the words would be taken seriously. Why ask a question? Why try to discuss things? Javier Castillo always seemed to know the answers, to have the answers. I would have had many questions for Mr. Castillo. At least I like to think that I would have had many questions. In reality, I would have spent, like Ricardo, far too much time wondering about how it all worked, the mechanics of it. But Ricardo? Ricardo went one step further in his thinking. Ricardo wondered if the affliction gave Javier Castillo special knowledge beyond that of travel, if somehow when in that space between disappearing and appearing there were answers. But this thought was too complicated for Ricardo to express. Despite trying to formulate the right questions to ask Javier Castillo, he simply remained silent. What he said to Javier Castillo, instead, was something about din-ner, about being incredibly hungry.

They left the track as the sun was setting, as the shadow time came into its own, people arriving at the track for the evening races still to come. As they walked through the parking lot, Ricardo felt the confusion in his chest flowering, growing larger and larger. Who was this man that held such sway over him? What was he? Were there others in the world capable of such things, others who were afflicted in this way? The questions came in rapid-fire succession, so much so Ricardo felt as if he simply appeared in the passenger seat of the car having little appreciation for having walked there from the stadium.

Ricardo and Javier Castillo went to the dingy Italian restaurant they frequented almost weekly. In the dimly lit restaurant with Frank Sinatra crooning softly through the hidden speakers, the backs of his arms sticking to the fake leather booth, Ricardo stared at Javier Castillo, smiled, but said nothing. Ricardo thought about ordering pasta, the kind that looked like little ears, but he couldn't for the life of him remember what they were called. Javier Castillo ordered that pasta for Ricardo without a single word passing between them. Yes, somewhere in that space between disappearing and appearing, there must have been answers, but Ricardo had no idea how one reached such a place without the affliction. The way Ricardo told it, it was then—the day he tested Javier Castillo—he began to worry, really worry. He worried one day in the not-too-distant future that Javier Castillo would go in search of answers and never return.

As he loved to recount Javier Castillo's disappearing acts, Ricardo also loved to recount how he first met Javier Castillo. He met him while working his evening shift at LAX. This, like the recollection of Javier Castillo's first disappearance, is a story I heard Ricardo tell many times, too many times really. To be honest, I still have doubts about this particular part of the story, but that is almost irrelevant now. Ricardo worked a second job each evening as a skycap. He would swap the grungy garage of the mechanic's for the grunge of LAX. In the gray space of the baggage claim, in the gray space of the check-in area, Ricardo had watched face after gray face arriving and departing. Javier Castillo was there to see his aunt off. Ricardo watched him the way he watched all people who were at LAX but neither arriving nor departing by plane. Accessories to travel, Ricardo had thought, accessories. They were not really people but means of transportation to or from the airport for these other people who were traveling by plane. He watched the backs of Javier Castillo and his aunt, watched as the aunt walked away. And when Javier Castillo turned around, Ricardo recounted how he felt a small shock, one he would never be able to fully explain.

As time passes, many people discover that what was not easily seen at one moment is suddenly easier to see later. Time is an excellent teacher in this way. But even after substantial time had passed, Ricardo could not explain why he had continued to stare at Javier Castillo that night. It was not that Javier Castillo was a handsome man. He was, in many ways, rather ordinary in appearance. He had dark brown, almost black, hair. His dark complexion was the color of *café con leche*, which made his gray-ish light brown eyes stand out. His nose was straight, almost hawkish. In all respects, except maybe the eyes, Javier Castillo looked like a version of the folks Ricardo saw every day. Javier Castillo looked squarely at him and said *"Buenas noches."*

They began to talk. Ricardo claimed he noticed the way in which Javier Castillo's eyes were light in color, noticed that his eyes were that pale brown flecked with gray. He always mentioned that, called atten-tion to that, as if such a thing as grayish eyes were something incred-ibly rare. That Javier Castillo had spoken to him in Spanish didn't sur-prise Ricardo. Many people spoke to him in Spanish, could tell from his features and dark skin that he was of Mexican descent. They exchanged small talk, nothing remotely exciting. And despite this, despite so little actually transpiring, Ricardo had felt his heart panic in his chest. He felt an incredible need to be with this man he had met only minutes before. Never before, in his life, had Ricardo felt this way. A man, he emphasized, he had never before felt this way about a man.

Despite Ricardo recounting this need, despite him telling the story of the evening he met Javier Castillo so many times, despite the fact I always wanted to know more about why he felt this way, Ricardo never added so much as a single extra detail. He simply acknowledged that for reasons unexplainable, even to himself, he felt the overwhelming need to leave with Javier Castillo, to follow him. Ricardo left the airport with him. He never went back. He never went home. He never called his wife and family. He couldn't think of what to say or how to explain Javier Castillo to them. He left the airport with him and drove for hours. In a corner of his mind, he believed he was being abducted, but he had not been abducted. He had asked Javier Castillo if he could come with him, something that surprised him as he posed the question. It was as if he were speaking without control of what he was saying. And in the sun visor mirror above him in the front passenger seat of Javier Castillo's car, Ricardo noticed his own eyes were a different color green. His eyes were more of a dark forest green, darker than the usual soft green he had seen in the mirror all of his life.

Once, after almost three years of living with Javier Castillo, Ricardo felt the sudden urge to press his hand through him just before he completely faded away. He wanted to see if he would also start disappearing. The affliction: what must it have felt like? Could Javier Castillo actually feel himself dissolving? The hands, finger by finger? But Ricardo knew that when Javier Castillo disappeared, he did so evenly. It was not as if the chest dissolved leaving the heart exposed and beating. He just slowly faded into a shimmer, and then a shadow, and then air. It was gradual. There would be a man, and then a man seen through but still there, and then the dingy, yellowed wallpaper clinging to the wall behind where Javier Castillo had been standing. Dingy and dirty: the wall would suddenly be more sharply in focus, its browning yellow like the nicotine-and-tar-stained filter after smoking a cigarette. And though Ricardo had no explanation, he knew the disappearing happened faster at times, more slowly at others. He wanted to pass his hand through the shadowy Javier Castillo, the one about to become air. But he could never get himself to do it. Oh, Ricardo thought about it. He thought about it many times. But Javier Castillo was always watching him carefully, and Ricardo feared that Javier Castillo knew what he was thinking. With Ricardo, there was always an element of fear.

What must such a life be like? Think about it. To live with a man half shadow, half something, something that you could not explain to someone else, much less yourself? Even after three years of living with Javier Castillo, after lying in bed next to him night after night, after sitting out on the small patio and smoking cigarettes, watching the smoke coil into shapes that only disappeared, Ricardo did not understand Javier Castillo. Ricardo never asked any questions. I have to believe if it were me in that situation I would have asked many questions or, better to say, I like to think I would have asked many questions. But Ricardo just didn't know how to do so. He lacked something: courage, determination, *fuerza*? I really couldn't tell you exactly.

Ricardo simply lived there with Javier Castillo, simply existed. He did not work. He did not worry about money. He didn't even worry about the wife and sons he left in the small neighborhood on the edge of nowhere. The time simply passed, and the man known as Javier Castillo moved in and out of the air. And finally that day arrived, the day that Ricardo could not recall with any great detail—Javier Castillo faded away and did not return. Even now, the fact Ricardo could not recall this day with even so much as a handful of details bothers me. Ricardo was no liar, but he must have remembered something, something more substantial than that the man named Javier Castillo simply disappeared and did not return. I have returned to this one moment so many times now, probably more times than Ricardo has, because it frustrates me; it troubles me to no end.

Ricardo thought nothing of Javier Castillo's disappearance at first. A week passed, and then a month. Ricardo had no money to pay the light bill or the utilities. He had no money to pay for anything. He had never questioned the fact that Javier Castillo always had money, was always able to pay for anything they needed. People seemed to just hand money over to Javier Castillo. Two whole months passed before Ricardo realized Javier Castillo was not coming back. Without electricity, Ricardo walked around the dark house occasionally flipping switches to see if something would happen. The air was dangerously still most nights, the heat of the desert coming in through the windows carried along by the echoing howls of the coyotes hunting in the nearby canyon. Ricardo was alone and without a dime. Within another day or two, he began to wander the streets. He did not remember how to go home to Rosa and his sons. He had no idea how to return to his *barrio* outside of Los Angeles.

He wandered for days, around town, across town. He wandered into the parking lot of the Travel Lodge just as I was stepping out of my rental car. Why he approached me, I will never really know. Maybe it was my dark complexion that marked me as one of *el pueblo*, the Latin look that offered a kind of safety to him that a white face could never offer. Maybe it was my responding to him in Spanish when he said *Buenas tardes*. I'm not sure. I don't usually talk to homeless people. It isn't that I am afraid of them, but that I have no idea what to say to them. But Ricardo's eyes were green, that dark forest green, and he looked haunted. I don't really remember exactly what I said to him, but he followed me, asked me if he could come up to my hotel room to take a shower, promised me he would not rob me.

I have no idea why I agreed. He showered and then came into the room and sat at the edge of the bed staring off into space. I offered him some whiskey—I always kept whiskey with me back then even when traveling—and we sat and drank it. I told him stories I had heard in my years of traveling as a salesman, told him stories of the small island in the Caribbean where I had grown up, the people there, the way we swore the cats were spies. We sat in our jockey shorts and t-shirts drinking whiskey. We lapsed into and out of Spanish. It seemed as if we had known each other for a very long time. At times, Ricardo would say he felt he knew this island where I had grown up, the place I had fled. He seemed to know some of the very names of streets and places, the docks and even the harbor. But I didn't think too much about this then. I didn't appreciate the strangeness of the fact he seemed familiar with these things, and many years would pass before I even remembered that.

Over the three months that followed, I heard much about Javier Castillo, too much, really: the disappearing, the timing of it, the various places he had visited. I had not actually seen Javier Castillo during those three months, but there were times when I felt quite certain I knew what he looked like. And Ricardo, though he never said so, sat sometimes cross-legged at the foot of the bed staring at the chair in my bedroom as if he were waiting for Javier Castillo to appear. Do I believe in gods? In angels? In miracles? No. No, I never have. I am more like Ricardo than I want to believe. Before he went to sleep most nights, Ricardo would say the very same thing to me. He would say: "Diego, sleep now. Sleep." Night after night, he said this, said it faithfully. And it made me wonder if he had instructed Javier Castillo to go to sleep in much the same way.

As time passed, night after night, lying in bed, Ricardo breathing deeply the way he did when he was lying down, I could not sleep. I found myself staring at the empty chair. I half-expected Javier Castillo to appear. I would love to be able to say now that I just wanted to make sure the chair was empty or, at most, the place where I left one of my old pairs of jeans. "Diego, sleep now. Sleep," Ricardo said. But falling asleep was the least of my concerns. I knew I would sleep eventually, much the way I knew, even then, that the day would come, that day where I might . . . I was concentrating so hard. I was concentrating on another place, another town. "Diego, sleep now. Sleep." Yes, even then the thought had entered my head: maybe I could disappear. Vanish, gone, in thin air, nothing left but the room, the bed, the chair. But I am no Javier Castillo, right? I am definitely nothing like Javier Castillo.

II. Inside the Great House

Crazy Old Cassie had been a nun. This much we all knew. This much could be verified. Almost every story about her began by referencing this fact. And there were far too many stories about this woman, too many for me to recount. I wouldn't even know where to start. The old men said the Archbishop placed her in the convent because she said she had seen the face of God. Men are always so romantic about these kinds of things. But women? No, they are the realists. The old women all said she had seen the face of the Devil. Some joked she had simply seen the other "face" of the Archbishop Castillo. Just as there were many variations on why Cassie was sent to the convent, no one could say with any certainty why she was eventually asked to leave it. But everyone knew Old Cassie was to be avoided. And she made it easy on us, very easy on us. She was rarely ever seen away from the Great House near the bottom of what we called Mutton Hill.

Old Cassie's real father, William Reynolds, had been a plantation owner. Some say he was the descendant of the bastard son of an English nobleman who had been exiled to the island to spare the family in England any embarrassment. When William Reynolds died, he left the estate and all the lands, the rum distillery, the orchards, the cattle ranch, all of it to his son and his son's family. But none of the Reynoldses who lived on the estate after William Reynolds died lived much longer than a few years. The old man died and then one by one his entire family followed his example. Accidents, sickness, and malady: that is what lived on that grand estate before Cassie did. And then the only person who lived there was Old Cassie. The only Reynolds still alive, alive even to this day, is

James Reynolds, the old Governor General, William Reynolds's brother.

The Great House kept watch over the town. If you looked north from the flea market or the town square, looked north and up the hillside, you would spy its large frame. There wasn't even another house near the bottom of that hill. The closest house was the Archbishop's Mansion that, despite looking close, was actually almost a mile away from the Great House. All of the land there, the entire hill, even beyond the hill deep into the center of the island, belonged to Cassie and her sister Flora once the Reynolds family died off. And Flora had long since left the island, moved somewhere in California, leaving all of it to Old Cassie.

Maria Consuela went to the Great House each morning to drop off milk and groceries, sometimes to straighten up the kitchen and the sunroom; she was usually gone by noon. She told others she rarely ever saw the old woman. The only person she ever saw in the house, and even that was rare, was Señora Grise, the woman she believed actually ran the house for Cassie. Maria Consuela would enter through the door on the side terrace and leave the items she brought on the kitchen counter under a purple-leafed plant hanging precariously in a wire basket. These were her standing orders. Once a week, Maria Consuela cleaned the kitchen, which meant wiping down the counters; the kitchen was never dirty. The floor tiles in the kitchen and sunroom always appeared spotlessly clean, almost as if no one actually lived in the Great House. And Derrick, the butcher's brother, went there twice a week to drop off major provisions, items he was told to leave on the wooden table on the back terrace. The field hands who worked the cane fields and orchards almost never laid eyes on Cassie and, at times, wondered if she really lived there; she rarely left the house. Cassie used to ride out to inspect their work, but with time it became more and more common for them to receive their orders by notes taped to the post at the bottom of the steps that led to the back terrace. Other than Maria Consuela, only cats entered and exited the Great House. Oh, there would be the occasional person who went there to seek help from the old woman, but Maria Consuela and Derrick were the only folks who dared to go there regularly. They had been chosen. They had been, in a sense, summoned.

People were usually warned not to look up at the Great House, even though this was a difficult task. It was the largest thing on any of the hill-sides, its hulking mass patiently watching over all of us. The old women made sure, almost daily, to warn us not to look up at that house. There was never even a hint of a joke when they said this. But how could one avoid looking up at it? One can stare out at the harbor with the sunlight shimmering on its surfaces for only so long before tiring. The one thing that gleamed in addition to that sunlit sea was the Great House, its white walls reflecting the sunlight like a beacon.

Occasionally, foreigners would arrive on large boats and ask about the house, ask if it were an inn made to look like an estate home, ask whether or not it was for sale. Tourists are so stupid sometimes. These foreigners wanted to actually stay there! But the only response any of us could give was that the house was "unsafe," at which these wealthy foreigners would look somewhat confused. They wanted to meet the owner, the innkeeper. They imagined this had to be an Englishman wearing tweed and riding apparel or sitting in a study sipping brandy while wearing a smoking jacket or an ascot. But this was not the case, and it hadn't been the case since the Reynolds family died off. There was no one there except Old Cassie. And she was certainly not an Englishman. No one on the island sought out that woman unless they absolutely had to do so. No one.

They say if Old Cassie looked you dead in the eye, she would know things about you, about your future. But Miss Simpson would laugh and say that sometimes people confused Cassie with her sister Flora, that it was the sister who could do that. But it didn't matter. What mattered was that we all feared Cassie, and Cassie probably liked it that way, or so we liked to believe. Miss Simpson once told me how many years ago, before Flora left, Cassie had cured a man of gangrene. She said the gan-grene was so bad the doctor had warned the man his leg would have to be amputated. Even then, it was unclear if that could save the man. No one remembers what Cassie actually did for the man, but she cured him. Apparently, as this man was leaving the house, Flora looked him dead in the eye while standing on the front porch and then pronounced that he would soon be wealthy but would lose it all. She told him he would end up flat out broke, without a single penny to his name. The man thought this was Flora's way of being foolish, which was a mistake in and of itself. He went to visit a relative in Miami a few weeks later. While there, he won the lottery: sixty-five million dollars.

He could have done anything he wanted to do on the island had he returned home. He could have built a big estate like the Reynolds Estate on one of the hillsides, could have owned a fleet of cars or boats. Hell, he could have owned just about everything the Church and the Reynolds Estate didn't already own. He would have been as wealthy as the Reynolds family had been. But he didn't come back. Well, not at first. He flew all over the world in private jets, stayed in unbelievable resorts, and ate only the finest foods. He lived a decadent life, a life of extravagance most of us cannot even imagine; but when he did return to the island, he was, in fact, broke. It was just as Flora had predicted, exactly as she had predicted.

In many ways, it was worse than she predicted; he actually owed money to a number of banks in America and Europe. It is just as likely he came home to the island to avoid the bankers finding him as much as the fact he was broke. In the grand scheme of things, it was easy to disappear from the eyes of the world by coming back to the island. No one in the world paid much attention to our small island in the Caribbean. What resources did we have to offer? Fish? The oceans are large and people can catch fish anywhere. Sugar cane? Rum? So many other islands offered up the same things and did so in far more abundance than we could. So what was the lesson here? What was the great teaching point? That you should be more careful with large sums of money? That you should invest and diversify your money? Save some of it? No, nothing like that at all. The lesson was that everything with those two sisters, whether you liked it or not, came at a price, sometimes a very steep price.

But as I was saying, Flora was long gone, leaving her sister Cassie to reign over all of us. And no one could say with certainty if having only one of those sisters around was any better than having both of them. Every morning, when Maria Consuela climbed part way up the hill to the Great House to drop off the groceries and clean up, the morning light, the sun behind the hill and the house, would litter the yard with shadows. The various shrubs and small manicured trees would throw long shadows across the walkways and paths. There, at the gate by the road, at the gate to the estate, she would see the decrepit royal poinciana tree that never seemed to grow. That stunted tree, at times covered in blood-red petals, always threw a shadow that resembled a rope hanging from it, a rope tied into a noose. This is no exaggeration. I have seen it myself. One of the shadows cast by the tree looks, for all intents and purposes, like the hangman's folly.

As she walked up the long drive or climbed the terraced steps up through the gardens, Maria Consuela would see the cats heading out. Twelve cats would leave the house and skulk off to various parts of the town. Sometimes, these cats went as far as three or four miles from the house. Miss Simpson told us the cats brought information back to Old Cassie, told us how both Cassie and Flora could communicate with cats. Miss Simpson warned us to be mindful of what was said if you saw one of those cats nearby. And Old Cassie did, in fact, seem to know everything that happened in the town. At least it seemed that way. She knew who was out at sea fishing, knew who was driving taxi, knew who was lifting one of the ever-more-present tourists' wallets. Nothing escaped her. For God's sake, not even the face of God had escaped her. From a distance, you could occasionally spy her rocking in a chair on her side terrace. She looked so kindly up there rocking in one of her chairs. But Miss Simpson is the first to remind you, lest you could forget, that there is nothing kind about that old woman, nothing remotely kind about her.

Miss Simpson had known Cassie since she was a child. They had been in grade school together. Miss Simpson said Cassie was incredibly smart in a way that frustrated the teachers. It seemed as if the girl never needed to study. It was as if she just absorbed information. It appeared effortless. Miss Simpson called her "scary smart," smart with maths, languages, history, science, everything. But she also admitted that Cassie was an arrogant girl. Cassie apparently told everyone she was going to be a doctor, a surgeon. But when Cassie's real father old man Reynolds died, his son and his son's family sent Cassie and her sister Flora to the convent. Flora eventually escaped the convent, but some of the old women claimed she was able to do so because Cassie cast a charm, put a spell on the ground-skeepers so they would come and let Flora out.

The story changed all the time. How could it not? Once Flora was no longer in the convent, even stranger things began to happen, terrible things. One by one, the entire Reynolds family who were still living in the Great House, the ones who had forced Cassie and her sister into the convent, became sick, or went mad. They all died. By the time Cassie left the convent a couple of years after her sister Flora did, no one was left at the Great House. And the Governor General's office turned the land rights, the rum distillery, and the Great House over to Cassie and Flora, the entire estate. Miss Simpson told us the Governor General turned it over to them because he was afraid of them, specifically Cassie. Cassie made people uncomfortable, even the Archbishop. Her half-brother, the younger Reynolds, the master of the estate then, hanged himself from the royal poinciana, the tree the Spaniards nicknamed the flamboyant tree, on the property near the gate, the very spot where Cassie's real father had hanged men who had stolen sugar cane, bananas, or other crops harvested from the estate's land. That beautiful royal poinciana tree was transformed into the very symbol of death, and many believe the tree refuses to grow because of all the terrible things it has seen.

Cassie, by dint of her real father, is related to the Governor General. James Reynolds is her uncle, a man born and raised in the Great House. *El pueblo* gossip he had no choice but to turn over the Reynolds Estate to Cassie to escape the calamity that seemed to be targeting his family. One never really knows the truth of these things. *El pueblo* gossip about the Governor General all the time. The Governor General, the Archbishop, Old Cassie: they make up the trifecta of gossip. But say what you want about Cassie; if a child were sick, or a woman were sick with child, she was the first one the women ran to for help. No woman would take her sick child or a relative in labor to the doctor. The doctor here studied in England. He is English. He carries the quiet disdain the English have for us. And too many children have died from his medicines and vaccines. Too many women have died in childbirth with him. The women all went to Cassie, instead.

I remember well the time when the doctor told Julia Esperanza, one of the grade school teachers, that her son had meningitis and that it was too late, told her the child's back had gone stiff and the fever was so high that all he could do was try to make the child comfortable. But Julia Esperanza picked up the child, carried him in her arms up the hillside road that circled the island, took him to the Great House, to Cassie. Cassie listened intently to the fearful voice of the grade school teacher, listened as she described how her son had gotten progressively sicker, how the doctor had said he would die. Julia Esperanza claims Cassie sat and listened, stood up, waved her hand and said "Foolishness!" She went outside and surveyed the yard, found the Scotch bonnet bush that was laden with the peppers, picked a faded orange pepper from the bush, brought it back inside and crushed it on the kitchen table with the bottom of a rum bottle before sprinkling its seeds into a tall glass of white rum. To this, she added a sprig of mint and some lavender dust before stirring the contents several times. She poured some of this in the then unconscious child's mouth and splashed some on his back. She stared at him. She stared at him so hard that had he been able to look back he would have been struck dumb with terror. She apparently screamed something in a language Julia Esperanza did not understand and then shook violently. When she stopped panting, after she had regained herself, Cassie told Julia Esperanza to take her son home, put him in bed, and then go outside and kill a young goat with her bare hands, to do it in the front yard. Cassie told her if she did this, the child would be fine.

Julia Esperanza took the boy home, put him in bed, and went outside to kill a young goat. As if instructed by an invisible shepherd, a young goat simply walked up to her and then sat down at her feet. It was difficult work, and she cried as did it. Julia Esperanza bawled, but she did it. She held the goat in her arms and quickly snapped its neck. It was much easier than she had imagined, the twisting of the small goat's neck and the way in which its body went limp after the terrible cracking sound. These things are always easier than people think. But the important part here is that she didn't dare disobey Old Cassie. And the boy was fine the next morning. The boy was as he had been before he had fallen sick: running around the front yard yelling and screaming, playing with branches to build miniature forts. And one less family on the island took their children to the English doctor.

Twelve cats roamed the town in the daytime, and twelve cats returned to the Great House each evening. Derrick, the butcher's brother, claimed Cassie named each cat after a noble region in Spain, told us how one cat was named Malaga, another Sevilla, and the mangiest one named Castilla, a fact that made many laugh considering the Archbishop's surname was none other than Castillo. Some nights, you could see a fire up there off to the side of the Great House. Other nights, the house and yard were pure darkness. Miss Simpson tells the story of how an old drunk at the beach bar joked he had bedded Cassie on the lawn outside the Great House by one of those fires. He joked Cassie was old and shriveled like a prune but that she was still a lusty and fiery woman more than capable of pleasing a man. You already know nothing good could have come of this.

A few days later, the drunkard's house caught fire. The blaze was spectacular, almost unearthly with the vigor in which it consumed the wooden house. People rushed to form a relay between the harbor and the house in an attempt to put the fire out. Bucket after bucket, the blaze remained insistent, but Miss Simpson was quick to point out that despite the fact other houses stood within mere feet of the blazing one, that despite the ever-present breeze that should have spread the blaze across the entire neighborhood, not a flicker of that fire strayed beyond the confines of its discrete burning. The drunk never made it out of the house. He was asleep, probably passed out from too much rum. We'll never know. Miss Simpson said that this is what happens when you talk like that about Old Cassie. Miss Simpson warned us all that Cassie knew, that she knew everything: "Call her crazy and mean, my boy. Call her what you like. But never disrespect that woman, Diego. If you disrespect her, it come at a very high price." Miss Simpson never joked when she said things like this. She meant it. Just like all the old women, she meant every word of it.

There were only five nuns left at the convent. There were other women that lived there, but they weren't nuns. Some of them dressed like nuns, but they could not be called Sister. Sister Juan Martín, the Reverend Mother, was the oldest of the nuns. She had come to the convent from Cuba as a young woman. She had entered the convent with Cassie and her sister, Flora. At the time, they were the first three women to come to the convent to become nuns in many years. Some say it had been a good ten years since any other women had come there to study and then take the vows. The Sisters ran the grade school and the high school, the hospital, and the flea market. They still do, even to this day. They fed and clothed the really poor, loaned money to fishermen who needed to repair boats. They were some of the only women that men lowered their heads to out of respect. Despite the fact no one paid an ounce of respect to the three priests on the island or Archbishop Castillo, men lowered their heads for the nuns.

Two of the three priests, along with the Archbishop, drank in the bar with all of the other men. They swore. They stumbled out of the bar at the end of the night drunk and disheveled. They were anything but celibate, and they sat and talked about women just like the other men. They were men first and men of God second. They spoke Spanish or English first and Latin second. As for the third priest, he was one of us, *el pueblo*, but he was a stern man, a bureaucrat, a numbers man rarely seen unless one went to the Archbishop's mansion. But the Sisters? No, they lived a life of devotion. If one of them came into the corner shop and ordered a soft drink, someone would run up and pay for it. If they ordered groceries, people would fork up money to pay for them. Even folks who had little money to begin with would sacrifice their last dime for those women. The Sisters never paid for anything. They were that good.

But Sister Juan Martín, yes, she had started at the convent at the same time as Old Cassie and her sister, Flora. And try as you might to get her to say something about her old compatriots, she wouldn't. She wouldn't say a single word. But honestly, no one ever asked her about Flora. Flora was gone, was somewhere in America. The one we all craved information about was Cassie. Sister Juan Martín would smile and say: "Now why would you want to hear about Cassandra?" It would sound like a question, but it was never a question. It was, in a way, a call to silence. You knew she was never going to say a word. I once heard Gran Señor

Murillo, the old *Cubano* who collects fees down at the docks, try to get Sister Juan Martín to say something about Cassie by addressing the nun by her birth name. But not even that worked. No amount of history or familiarity could get her to say a bad word about Cassie. The Sisters never spoke ill of anyone, not even Old Cassie. But that didn't stop folks from trying to get them to do so.

Teenagers back then used to sometimes joke that Old Cassie probably left her house in disguise and that she might well be standing near the Spanish fountain or sitting over by the market near the square. This was done just to scare other kids; it was difficult not to talk about Old Cassie. She came up daily, the way the weather comes up in conversation. The weather here is almost always the same: hot, muggy, breezy some of the time, but everyone talks about it anyway. It was the same with Cassie. People wondered what she did with all of that money she had, the land behind the Great House, the house itself. They wondered what she ate, if she drank the rum from the estate's distillery, if she ever went on holiday. People couldn't help it. They talked about her all of the time, stopping only because they spied a cat nearby.

Miss Simpson told us that Cassie actually started medical school. She was the only woman in her medical school class in England. Miss Simpson said Cassie's real father, old man Reynolds, was strangely proud of how smart Cassie was. She was first in her class in high school. She was studying medicine when old man Reynolds died. The Reynolds family refused to continue paying for Cassie once William Reynolds was placed in the ground, told her to come home to the Island to help out at the Great House. Cassie had no other family. Her mother was old and sick then, too sick to help her or anyone else. The man we all originally thought was Cassie's father died mysteriously several years before that in an accident one morning as he took his boat out, something involving him getting caught in his own net and being dragged quickly down into the sea and drowning, the weight of his body in the net anchoring the boat in the harbor for days before anyone realized what had happened. But even before that, old man Reynolds had taken Cassie and Flora as his charges, and with time it had become known that he had fathered them both, that he had slept with their mother Tita Diaz, the healing woman.

When Cassie received the orders from the Reynolds family to come home after old man Reynolds died, she did. She had no choice. Not even Miss Simpson knows exactly what happened in the Great House in the time after the old man's death, but it had to have been bad. Cassie and Flora did not go to the convent of their own free will. Many seem to know that aspect of the story. They were forced into the convent by their half-brother and his wife. Cassie had done something terrible, but no one seemed to know or remember what it was she had done. One never questioned a "half-milk" like Cassie or Flora, and one definitely never questioned the "milk-bread," what the old people called the full English like the Reynolds Family. You could question *el pueblo* or the Indians or the blacks, but you never questioned a "milk-bread" or a "half-milk." You never so much as looked one of them directly in the face. What we know is the Reynolds family had proclaimed that Cassie and Flora could no longer live in regular society and that they had the two of them hidden away at the convent. Maybe they believed God and His Holy Church could change them, save them, perhaps. We will never know.

But you already know what happened. All of the Reynolds family, one by one, died. Cassie's half-sister-in-law tripped and broke her ankle, stumbled and fell into a ditch. They took her to the doctor and he splinted her ankle. She limped. She was in pain. Men were called from the streets to help carry her back to her car. But then, on her way home, a tree branch fell and hit the car. Some even say it was a branch from the shak shak tree, the flamboyant tree by the entrance to the Great House, that fell on the car. The driver lost control, swerved and ended up going over the embankment to plunge headlong into the sea. The sea's many layers swallowed the car whole. Both she and her driver, if they weren't already dead, drowned. You can still find the spot where the car left the road in its lunge for the sea; a small white wooden cross is staked in the dirt there on the side of the road that circles the island, planted not too far from the entrance to the Reynolds Estate.

Both of Mrs. Reynolds's children died mysteriously. A frightened horse kicked the girl in the back of the head, and she was found dead on the speckled gray gravel out near the stables behind the Great House, the blood pooled like a lopsided halo around her crooked head. The boy died in an accident out in the fields, his body hidden carefully in the sugar cane for almost two weeks. And, well, you know what happened to Old Cassie's half-brother, the younger Mr. Reynolds. He hanged himself in the front yard by the gate to the Estate, hanged himself from a branch of the stunted royal poinciana tree standing guard there, his body swinging for all to see when the morning light crept over the hill behind the Great House.

It is never easy to know a story well. Sometimes, all one can gather is an impression. Sometimes, Time itself muddies the details to the point little if any fact remains. The younger Mr. Reynolds saw ghosts, some say, saw his own dead father beating one of the children to death. The younger Reynolds was sick and told by the doctor he would die a slow and agonizing death. The younger Reynolds was heartsick after the loss of his wife and children. The younger Reynolds wanted to test out a wild theory about reincarnation. None of these is true, and yet they are all true. Miss Simpson told us the younger Mr. Reynolds was a weak man and that he was simply too weak to withstand the curse left on the land by Old Cassie and her sister Flora. But none of that branch of the Reynolds family remains to confirm or deny any of this. None of them can tell us what happened between Old Cassie and the younger Reynolds and his wife. All that is left is the Great House and the land. All that is left is silence.

Old Cassie watched over us all from the Reynolds Estate. She had all of their money and all of their land. She had their standing, the people afraid of her much the way they had feared the Reynolds family for almost a century. *El pueblo* call up their best English when they address her, if they dare to address her. But no one called Old Cassie a Reynolds. No, she was something else altogether. Miss Simpson said that people from abroad sometimes came to the island for her help: sick people, really sick people, dying people. And Cassie spoke to them in their own languages; she knew English, Spanish, French, German, Hindi, and *Patois*. She even knew Chinese and Portuguese.

How the foreigners found her, how they found out about her, is anyone's guess. The say that when the Governor General's favorite young housekeeper was sick with pneumonia, the fever so high the girl had become delirious, he reluctantly took her to Old Cassie. We have no way of knowing what she did exactly, but she cured the girl of her illness. Even to this day, *el pueblo* claim this is why the Governor General turns a blind eye to the odd things that happen on the grounds of that old estate. One wonders what the Sisters would have done if one of them were to become sick. Would they have gone to Old Cassie? Would that even be possible?

But they never had reason to go to Cassie. Those women were never sick. Even now, they are never sick. They remind us that cleanliness is next to Godliness. They moved around as if their feet were cautiously floating above the ground beneath those habits. They prayed for our souls and our bodies. They made sure things got done. They listened to us and cared for us. And Cassie? She crushed a whole pepper in the bottom of a glass and added hot water. She drank this the way many of us drink tea or coffee. She sometimes rocked in her chair on the side terrace of the Great House. She gathered her evidence and her information. And was she ever sick? Did she ever need care? Back then, no one could have predicted. What the women did, what they did faithfully, was to pray for her. They lit candles at Santa María Estrella del Mar and prayed to the Madonna. They prayed for the woman who saved their sick children, the woman who helped them give birth, the woman they all believe saw the face of the Devil and lived.

III. The Experiment

There were those who had survived the experiment, and those who had not. Of this, I am certain. This is the one aspect I know to be true, having heard it a number of times. Although there was no name assigned to either category of people, everyone who lived in Silas fell into one of two camps: the ones who had survived the experiment, or the other, the ones who had not yet been subject to the experiment. It had always been this way. No one, I am told, talked about what happened to those who had failed the experiment. No one even used the word "experiment." That term is my own, invented purely as a way to discuss it.

Three generations lived in the town of Silas, a town shrouded by large overarching trees that brought new meaning to the word "canopy." Instead of clearing the trees to build their small homes, the people of Silas had built among the trees, the only small clearing made for their central square. There was the lone old man who was almost one hundred years old. No one ever thought to ask the nonagenarian if things had always been this way. It would have been easier to ask him if he had eaten breakfast that morning or if he was fasting for the week. The tourists who stopped on the hill road miles away to look down at Silas through binoculars knew only that this was a town that was unlike any other town in Spain, that there was no road into the town and, conversely, no road out. They could see the small central square and the tops of trees. The houses, small as they were, were not visible from that height and distance, the trees' branches and leaves interwoven as if by design to keep the town virtually invisible.

The way Leenck told it, Silas was more than a town; it was a character in the story itself. Silas, where the butcher had eaten all the fish in one night, where the people spoke a language that sounded at times like Spanish but was a language those of us who knew Spanish could not really understand, the town where the children all lived in a single large house away from their individual families until the age of sixteen: the tour guides knew none of these things and, instead, made up many one-liners for Silas, one-liners that were recited in a dry, matter-of-fact way that filled the tourists with something like wonder. Busload after busload, made up primarily of people traveling on cruise ships who had chosen an excursion that took them inland away from the port, stopped either on the way in or the way out to stare down at this town that was barely visible and that barely seemed worthy of a mention. Tourists: they seemed to multiply. Tourists kept appearing all over the world to watch and pass judgment on what could be seen or, in this case, what could not be seen. It didn't matter if the place were a small island in the Caribbean or a small town buried in the woods outside Barcelona. There were tourists and tour guides and the unfortunate people and places they looked upon with a mix of pity and, yes, wonder.

But none of the tour guides referred to the experiment. How could they? I cannot imagine they knew anything about it. Day after day each summer, in early afternoon, the sunlight harsh and unforgiving as it can be at that time of year, the buses with their hordes would stop up on the hillside road to look down at Silas from the lookout point clearly constructed for this purpose and this purpose only. There was no other reason for such a lookout to exist on that country road far from the city. And the children of Silas would disappear from the Square each day about a half hour before the buses arrived. The tourists were never to see the children of Silas. The women of the town made sure of that. They frightened the children with tales of abductions, of this child or another that many years ago had been taken from the town. Like clockwork, they would come out of their houses and rush the children inside when they knew the buses were coming.

The way Leenck explained it, he was sixteen when everything changed. He had just reached the age at which he could move back home with his family. At the home for children, he slept in a room only 8 x 8 feet, a room with no windows that he shared with another boy. Trust me, I remember this all very well because it seemed so completely different from the way I had grown up. Yes, *el pueblo* on the island watched over the children in general, but nothing they did seemed remotely like what Leenck had described to me. None of the rooms in the children's house in Silas had windows. The entire building had no windows, and each room's door locked from the outside. Leenck's job then, after he had come home, was to gather wood for the stoves and, sometimes, to help his father clean and sharpen the greater axe, a monstrously large axe with a blade so brilliant you could use it as a mirror.

Leenck had watched his father and uncle use the greater axe. It was reserved for the larger trunks of trees, its purpose being to make a clean slice through limbs or trunks for which a lesser axe would have had difficulty. He knew at some point he would learn to use the greater axe, to "wield it" as his father and his Uncle Pitro said. And Leenck understood that at some point he would have to endure the experiment. Endure: the very word his father and uncle used when they brought up the experiment. One or both of them would bring up this feat, but neither would ever say much about it. The experiment was always discussed in this way: endurance. The experiment was a test of endurance. Other than that, Leenck knew very little about it then. He did not know the type of endurance that would be necessary. For all he knew, it would be a physical challenge, a race or feat such as climbing the tallest tree in Silas. But if he had thought more carefully, he would have realized that he had never seen or heard of anything like a race or a challenge to climb a tree. The experiment took place out of sight. And he feared, for good reason, that one was never the same after the experiment.

Leenck's family knew nothing about life outside of Silas. They didn't know about money or politics, at least not the kind of politics that went on in the country around them. They talked about the outside world in hushed voices, as if to even discuss anything outside of Silas was to invite the wrath of God. There was no Franco, no Juan Carlos, no regimes or fallen empires. There was no obsession with the fashions of the wealthy aristocrats, whether of noble family or not. There wasn't even a strong sense that the country around them was Spain. People in Silas knew there were hunters, butchers, growers, weavers, etc. There was the nonagenarian who gave advice, and the old woman the children knew as the teacher, the woman who presided over the children's home. People had roles and tasks, both at home and for the town, but little else.

The nonagenarian and the teacher both knew stories and recited them at certain times of the year such as the solstices and after the big harvest. And Leenck figured he would be a builder like his father, one who wielded the greater axe and fashioned wood into objects for others. When he lived with the children, he knew little about his family except for the fact that his family worked as the builders. That is what men in his family did. He had no idea what the women in his family did, though he knew one of the women who cared for the children was a relative of his, an aunt or second cousin. His best friend, a year younger and still living with the children, was a milker; his family kept the cows and made the butter and cheese. But ahead of Leenck back then was the experiment and little else. Despite the fact his mind tried and tried to latch itself to something concrete for the experiment, nothing concrete ever presented itself.

Early one morning, just before sunrise, with only a slight tint of light and a darkish blue in the sky, Leenck claimed he remembered hearing people outside his parents' home. Leenck wasn't even completely sure he was awake. As he lay on his cot then with the flimsy woven blanket covering him, he heard a woman's voice saying something about not being ready. He thought for a minute or so that he was dreaming. It had to have been a dream because that many people would not have been outside so early. The milkers were up that early and, sometimes, a select group of others. But there were many voices, this he remembered, and the sound of people moving about. He heard a woman scream out "No." It was a gut-wrenching scream filled with an anguish Leenck had never heard before. And he knew then quite certainly it was no dream.

He swung his legs over the side of the cot and ran to the small window in his room at his parents' house. He saw, moving away from the Square, a group of people slowly making their way past the butcher's place and the children's home and toward the eastern edge of the town, toward the Dark Forest, the part of the surrounding forest so dense children were warned not to enter it. Again, he heard the woman scream out "No." He couldn't figure out who among the group was screaming. And it occurred to him the woman screaming might well have been off to the side of the group he could see moving then into the Dark Forest. The scream echoed in the Square and off the walls of the tiny houses. All Leenck knew was that he felt nervous, squeamish, and that he had goose bumps along his arms and that the tiny hairs on the back of his neck seemed to be bristling. His stomach grumbled, and he felt nauseated. The nausea would pass, and later, when his parents came back, he knew, without understanding why, that his parents Las and Mencka had been in that group of people herding someone toward the Dark Forest.

"Unexplainable things happen all of the time, Diego," Leenck would say. "Usually, as time passes, these things grow to seem ordinary. With time, one thinks back and wonders how one could have misunderstood what was clearly such a simple thing." Even then, I had no real understanding of this story of his. But he would continue on, dutifully, as if the story itself were a wonderful betrayal. It was told with that kind of wink. The bus drivers who stopped to show tourists the town of Silas in the distance; the fact there were no roads in or out of the town; the nonagenarian: all would be understandable at some point in the future. Or so I wanted to believe. Would Leenck ask his father what had happened in the Square that morning? Of course not. Leenck was more afraid of the answer than of asking the question. And buried inside his mind, among his ever-wandering thoughts, Leenck probably knew what had happened that morning. He knew back then he would some day be in the same position, and he hoped his mother would not scream out "No!"

*

"I think the boy is ready."
"Don't rush him. He's still so young."

"I just have that feeling. You understand?"

"Damn it, Las, just because you did it at a young age doesn't mean he is ready. Our father, were he alive, would not push him. He didn't push you."

"The boy is more like me than you think, Pitro. You haven't seen him use a hatchet or a sentient knife."

"Yes, but remember he has to be ready. He has to be ready up here." As he said this, Pitro quickly pointed to his head.

"Is any one of us really ready for it?"

"I was almost twenty-two before I did it. And I am not sure I would have made it out had I gone in any earlier."

"He is ready. I just know it. He has that look and that way about him."

"I am not his father. But you should talk to Mencka before you put him up for this."

"Mencka doesn't watch him the way I do."

"Yes, but she is his mother. Mothers know. They know things."

"Stop worrying. You sound like an old woman yourself."

"Don't let pride push you to the point you damage your only son."

"He is ready. I'm telling you, he is ready. I can feel it."

"Have you forgotten our brother? Father thought Ysinck was ready. Father learned this lesson the hard way with him . . ."

"Ysinck was weak. He was never one of us."

"He was our brother! He wasn't weak. He just wasn't ready."

"When would he ever have been ready? When he was forty? Fifty? He was thirty years old when he was taken to the cell!"

"He wasn't thirty. He was twenty-seven, but he was still too young, and Father never forgave himself. He wasn't ready. Pride. You went to the cell so early, Father thought we all could."

"Ysinck never had the look. He was always afraid. Afraid of the axe. Afraid of the knife. For God's sake, he was afraid of the wood!"

"Was he though? Or was he simply not meant to be a builder?"

"Now you really sound like an old woman. We are builders. We are not butchers or weavers or anything else. We are placed here to build. We were born to be builders. Leenck is a builder. He's one of us. He understands. I swear to you, I can tell."

"Is he? Is he a builder, or do you want him to be so badly you . . . "

"Yes. I know it. I am his father. I can tell."

"I really hope so, Las. Mencka would never forgive you. Just like Mama never forgave Father."

"I will speak with her. I will speak with her soon."

"You have to . . ."

"You will see."

"Leenck is all we have. Between us, there are no other boys in this family. All we have are girls. We have to be sure. One of our brothers did not survive the cell, and our youngest brother disappeared in the Dark Forest when he was a young boy. He was never able to prove himself!"

"I am sure. Of course, I am sure."

"Leenck is all we have now. Speak with Mencka. See what she thinks about . . ."

"I will! I will speak with her and see what she thinks. If she just watched the boy working with me, she would know. He is ready. He will survive."

*

In the east, I was told, roughly two miles into the Dark Forest, buried partially underground, was the cell. The cell was 8 feet x 8 feet, a concrete-walled room with no windows. It had one oil lamp hanging from a wire, hanging from the very center of the ceiling. One oil lamp, probably a hundred years old, hung there giving off a yellowish, old-papery light. There was one small vent at the center of the ceiling to allow smoke to clear the room. There was one iron door with a handle and latch on the outside only, a small path sloping upward to the level ground of the field halfway up its walls. Perfectly square, this room. And in the left-hand corner of this square room, when standing in the doorway looking in, in the left-hand corner near the ceiling was a small spigot. And below the spigot on the ground, a small bowl, a soup bowl, which caught the rusty-orange water that dripped from the spigot. The water never poured from the spigot, it just dripped. The spigot was placed close to the ceiling so one could not reach it to turn off the water. One drop every twenty or so seconds. When the bowl had some of the rusty-orange liquid in it, *chulp*. When the bowl was empty, *plink*. If one removed the bowl from beneath the spigot, *plesh*. Otherwise, there was no sound in the room. The light did not hum or buzz. There was no bed, no furniture, nothing but the floor and the four walls. And in the center of the room, on the floor directly beneath the oil lamp, a drain with a crosshatched rusted metal grate over it, into which the rusty-orange liquid could be poured or, if the bowl overflowed, the rusty-orange liquid would find by way of gravity. The floor, although it appeared flat, was actually a conical thing. The floor sloped ever so slightly down toward the drain, the angle of slope only visible to the eye when water was poured in one of the corners of the room because the liquid would then slowly make its way toward the center. You could watch the liquid crawl toward the room's center, toward the drain. The iron door did not touch the ground. There were four inches of space at the bottom, enough for a tray to slide under, or a rat, enough to see the shoes of anyone who stood outside the iron door. It was enough for air to move in and move out. Leenck recalled all of this with what seemed an incredible accuracy.

*

"The axe is an extension of your shoulders and back. Your arm is only a part of the axe's handle. When held correctly, the axe moves with the body as if a part of the body. Your center is the source of its strength. The swing starts here and moves up the back and through the arm until the axe finds its target. Do you see?"

Leenck watched and listened to his father. And Leenck knew his father watched him but never listened to him. When his father pulled string around the trunk of a tree, Leenck would study exactly how far from the ground the string was tied, would note which side of the tree his father brought the axe to strike. It was easy for Leenck to notice these kinds of things. He had no explanation for why he so easily noticed and understood these things. And when his father stripped down at the end of the day to check himself for splinters, Leenck would do the same.

"Why do we gather wood from the forest in every direction except the East?"

"We do not cut down trees from the Dark Forest."

"But why? The trees there are huge and could provide a lot more wood."

"The Dark Forest cannot be touched, Leenck."

"It just seems odd that we ignore the woods to the East."

"It is not for you to question these things but to understand."

It had been a long day in the forest and, to impress his father, Leenck decided to tie a string around his thigh to show his father that he understood how far up a trunk to cut. But there was no string available in the room, so Leenck used a fine metal wire, the type one used to tie through and cut small branches so as not to kill the tree. But the knot was too good of a knot, the wire too tight, and the leg below the knee started to swell. It swelled until it brought tears to Leenck's eyes. He stood before his father, naked, with his leg swollen and turning a white then a purplish-blue color. His father said almost nothing except that he had, in fact, tied the wire at the right spot for a trunk that matched the thickness of his thigh. Within twenty minutes, Leenck could no longer feel his toes. They had gone from tingly and prickly to numb and then cold. His father was already dressed for the remainder of the evening, but all Leenck could do was put on a shirt. He was afraid to pull up his under shorts or pants because of his leg. And he began to worry. He slumped to the floor while leaning against the wall. It all seemed to be happening in slow motion, his body slowly descending to the gravelly ground, the rough wall scraping his back as he did so.

Leenck didn't really know his father well. He had rarely seen him in the years he lived with the children. On holidays, he would sit with his family and listen to the stories. And what he knew of his grandfather was essentially what others knew, that he was a builder, that his father and his father's father were builders, and that the sons in the family were builders. His grandfather had four sons: his father; his Uncle Pitro; the reviled Ysinck who brought the family shame; and his Uncle Axick, who at five years of age wandered into the Dark Forest never to be seen again. For all Leenck knew, all the men in his family were builders. They must have all possessed the skills for taking wood and making of it the things people in the town needed: cabinets, chairs, tables, bowls, the polished wooden plates used at dinner on the solstices. Leenck thought about this as tears began to run down his face. The leg hurt. It hurt more than he had ever imagined anything could hurt. And his father stood there calmly watching him.

"You tied it too tight, son."

"I didn't mean to, but . . . "

"Can you loosen it at all?"

"I have, I have tried, but now I can't move my leg."

"You are in pain? Is it terrible?"

"I can't feel my toes."

"Well, we will have to amputate the leg. There isn't a thing more we can do."

"What?"

"Chop it off before it gets so bad it takes you."

"Chop it off?"

"Stay here. I will go get the greater axe."

Leenck could only do as his father said. He could not have gotten up and walked much less run—the leg now an almost pale-white, the purplish color fading while the leg felt as if it were on fire. It looked, to Leenck, to be almost twice the size of his other leg, but the mind is so good at exaggeration that the leg was only mildly larger than the one he had not tied off. He was lying on the ground with only a shirt on after tying a wire around his leg, just above the knee. And he was embarrassed. Not because he was naked, not even because he had tied the string too tight. He was embarrassed because he knew he had let his father down. In his excitement to show what he had learned, he had done something incredibly stupid. How would he be able to do the experiment with one leg? He would never become a builder now. He knew this. He knew he would disappear like the others who had failed the experiment. Or worse, he would spend the rest of his life never being able to do the experiment, something that seemed unfathomable to Leenck.

As he thought this through to its end, his father returned. He was carrying the greater axe. He held it by the edge of the handle so that the full weight of the axe hung down perfectly perpendicular to the ground. It didn't swing because of its weight and the slow methodical way his father moved.

"Can you slide down on the floor so you are lying flat?" His father leaned the axe against the wall Leenck was leaning against so that out of the corner of his eye he could see the light reflecting from its smooth sharpened surface. "Can you shift yourself forward?"

Leenck knew he couldn't but found it difficult to tell his father this fact. It was just another instance in which he felt ashamed, felt as if he were disappointing his father and his father's expectations. He kept trying to find the right words but found, instead, nothing. It was as if his lips were suddenly tied together with a metal wire or had been sewn shut with catgut.

"Leenck!" his father shouted, "Can you shift forward enough to lie flat? I need you flat so I can make a clean cut."

"No. No, I don't think I can."

His father stepped forward, placed one hand under Leenck's back, the other on his shoulder, and then both lifted him slightly and moved him forward until he was flat on his back, the heels of his feet pushing the gravelly ground as he went flat. Now there were small mounds of gravel just beyond his feet. His father had only the axe with him, no towels or sheets. Nothing else. And Leenck could feel the gravelly floor beneath his backside. He could see an insect of some kind through the corner of his eye scramble up the leg of a nearby chair. Lying there on the ground, his father looked monstrously tall. Leenck had never noticed how big a man his father was until then. "This is going to hurt, Leenck. But it is necessary. You understand that, right? You will have much less pain in the end. In the long run, you will have much less pain."

Leenck said nothing in response. The tears had stopped, but now he could feel his heart in his chest in a way he had never appreciated before. His heart jerked and raced so hard he worried it would burst from his chest. His father picked up the axe. "I want you to take a deep breath and hold it. Can you do that?"

Leenck did as his father said. His heart, beating madly then, seemed even more pronounced as he held his breath. And within seconds, he saw the axe swing high above his father's head, the arc of it moving above and away from him. And then the arc reversed and he watched as the axe, swift from its own weight and the power of his father's arms, came down. He heard the loud hatch sound as the axe entered the ground. And he expected to see blood, expected to see his leg rolled onto its side away from his thigh. But when he looked down, he saw the axe in the ground about three inches to the side of his leg. His father's face was flat. His forehead was smooth. Not a movement could be found near his eyes or mouth. "The leg! You missed!" Leenck cried out.

"I did not miss. I hit the target exactly." His father walked over to the door and picked up a machete. He came back toward Leenck and slid the machete under the wire so that only about two inches of it passed under the wire. He gave a quick jab and twist and the wire snapped. When the wire fell on either side of his leg, Leenck realized there was a trickle of blood coming from a small, roughly 1-cm puncture in his thigh above where the wire had been tied, where the point of the machete had quickly entered the meat of his thigh. Leenck could still see the impression of the wire on his thigh, could show exactly where the wire had circled his thigh even many years later. The tip of the machete had just punctured the skin, but the small hole bled and bled. "Something to remind you," his father said.

It took almost six minutes before Leenck could stand up on his leg. After he got up, he put on his undershorts and pants. He looked at his father, but got no response from him. His face gave nothing to Leenck. It was without feeling or reaction, as it had been throughout the entire terrible episode. And Leenck felt ashamed. He had never before felt such a deep and overwhelming sense of shame. His heart was still not right in his chest. The shame spread from his chest to his face. And he walked out of the room to go help his mother fire the stove. After Leenck left the room, you can almost imagine his father smiling and then mumbling out loud, something like "He *is* ready."

IV. The Fortunate

Some are good at digging up the past, and some are gifted with the ability to divine the future. Most people live squarely in the present without even the slightest knowledge that all of time coexists, that each era is simply a thin rind circling the current moment. Rosa Blanco was one of those people who lived in the present, but she was always obsessing about the past and worrying about the future. In her small kitchen, she would, sometimes for hours, replay a moment in the past, ten, maybe fifteen, times. Each time, she checked and rechecked what she had said, how she had said it, what she had done. But the old woman who lived a few doors away was a different type of woman. She lived for the future.

I won't explain how I came to hear this part of the story. At this point, it is almost irrelevant. But suffice it to say, once you hear it you never forget. You keep it, embellish it, turn it over and over in your head like a cloudy gem you have been asked to examine and appraise. But it starts with Rosa Blanco. It all starts with Rosa Blanco. In many ways, that woman is responsible for everything, the way I see it. I fault her. I fault her for pretty much all of it. But let me explain further. I need to explain further. Rosa Blanco was intent on knowing how the old woman divined the future. She wanted to understand the mechanics of it, the exact ways in which she could open the future up in front of her like an old book. She was certain, quite certain, that the old woman did not use tea leaves or a crystal ball. She had asked her once about tea leaves, and the only response she had gotten was something about water dissolving what power they had.

The old woman simply never used tea leaves. It wasn't that she despised vegetable matter, but that she relied on it, relied on it to see things.

Threads, she called them. The old woman would take the dried leaves of plants people brought to her and then use them to her own devices. What Rosa Blanco knew, from the slight lilt to the old woman's voice, was that she was not originally from Mexico or a daughter of Mexico. Rosa Blanco never asked, but she believed, and rightfully so, that the woman had been born in the Caribbean. Her Spanish was not Puerto Rican, but it may have been Dominican. The clipping of the "r" when she spoke Spanish made Rosa Blanco suspicious, but she dared not ask the old woman to tell her from where she had come. To Rosa, that would have been rude. I would not have needed to ask, would have recognized that accent almost immediately. It is, after all, the very same one I hear from my own mouth when I speak Spanish, as rare as that is.

The first time Rosa Blanco visited the old woman was one of those moments she must have replayed over and over in her head for the rest of her life. Carmen Jiménez, the cashier at the grocery store, told Rosa Blanco how she had visited the old woman, told her that the old woman had looked into her future, and that she told her she would soon be pregnant. A month later, Carmen Jiménez visited her doctor and was told she was with child. Rosa Blanco had heard other stories like this. She had heard, in fact, many stories like this. All of them ended with the old woman's predictions coming true. And why Rosa Blanco had gone to see the old woman that day, why she let her curiosity rule her mind, was the piece of cloth she crumpled and then smoothed out over and over again in her mind for the rest of her life.

Rosa Blanco obsessed about the past. So what possessed her to seek out the future is the aspect of all of this I will never understand. Somewhere inside her, I would wager, she believed the old woman actually made these predictions happen. She would spend every day of her remaining life blaming the old woman for her problems, and yet, she was always thinking about when she could go to visit her, when she could find some time to ask her what was coming, what to expect. Despite all of that longing to know the future, Rosa Blanco only sought out her own future exactly three times. Difficult to believe, but true.

The old woman came from a blessed family, Rosa Blanco had been told, a family that understood the ways in which herbs and plants worked. Rosa Blanco still wanted to believe that she first went to see the old woman because a crocus plant near her back door had died, suddenly, giving off a terrible odor that lingered long after the dead plant was pulled from the ground and burned. She believed this with all her soul, that she went to her to find out why this had happened. But the past was not what the old woman held in her hands. When Rosa Blanco knocked on Flora Diaz's door, there was a long pause before she heard the old woman walking to the door. When the old woman opened the door, she looked suspicious. She invited Rosa Blanco in and offered her a seat with a wave of her hand only. She offered her lemon water. And then she told her that she wasn't ready for her, that she had expected her to come but that she was not ready. Rosa Blanco wanted to feel startled, but didn't. The old woman went on to say she had been expecting Rosa Blanco to come to her in about two weeks' time.

It wasn't as if the old woman brandished a wand over spilled water and then fell into a trance, her eyes open but glazing over. No, it was nothing like that at all. It was all very scientific. She needed things. She needed the leaves of a plant, and she needed them to be dry, brittle, desiccated. Without the leaves, Flora told her, the ability to see the future clearly would be hindered. And so, when Rosa Blanco asked the old woman if there was anything she needed to tell her, the only response she got was a curt negative. Rosa Blanco had no idea then what to do, so she just sat there and waited to see what the old woman would say. The old woman talked about her family, how her family had been an important family for centuries, how they were the healers, the keepers of the gifts, the ones who tended the plants not for food but to keep the people on her island anchored in time. She rambled on to Rosa Blanco about how at any one time there were at least three women in her family that kept the gifts, kept the gifts alive. Rosa had no idea what the old woman was talking about, but she listened all the while hoping something about her own future would be revealed.

The old woman went on and on, told her how everything changed when the ghosts arrived on their ships, how they killed off many of the men on the island, raped the women, took the land. It was then she chuckled, a strange little laugh, before stating that these ghost men had no idea the power of the land, the plants that grew from the land, or the women that tended the plants, that no matter how ambitious and sonorous their Spanish language was it would never erase the language and power of the land. Rosa Blanco could not follow what the old woman was saying then, but she continued to listen. She couldn't help but listen. She felt as if she could not rise from her chair and walk out. The old woman continued, told her that the original ghost men thought that time and successive generations would erase her family's gifts, but that this never happened. "Every girl born to us carried it!" The old woman laughed some more and then offered Rosa Blanco more lemon water. "Every one of them! Most would never realize the full power of their gifts. But there were always at least three who would . . ." Rosa Blanco declined the water and finally told the old woman she needed to go home and start cooking dinner. As she stood up from the table, Rosa Blanco saw a wire basket filled with orange-colored peppers.

"What kind of peppers are those?"

"They have no name. The Spaniards called them *los calientes*. The English called them Scotch bonnets. I have a man back home mail me a box of them each week."

"Peppers? But they sell them at the store."

"Not those peppers. I crush one each morning into a glass and pour hot water over it. I sip a glass of the infused water every morning. It clears the head, clears the mind and the body, prepares the body . . ."

There was no doubt that the old woman, Flora Diaz, was an odd woman. And Rosa Blanco was sure then that she was not from Mexico, not from the country that birthed most of the people in the area, Mexico with its insistent puppy dog love of Spain and all things Spanish, its ignorance of the people who had lived there long before the arrival of the *Conquistadores*. But before Flora Diaz could say any more about the peppers, the strange breakfast, the clearing of the mind, the old woman said: "Next time, bring me leaves. Pull them from a plant in your yard and set them in the sun to dry. When they are dry and brittle, bring them to me.

Then I will be able to tell you what it is you need to know."

It took Rosa Blanco two weeks before she returned to see Flora Diaz. In that time she had gone outside and pulled leaves from the crocus plant next to the spot where the dead one had been. She had put them on the sill in the kitchen window to dry. When her husband, Ricardo, had asked her about the leaves drying up and browning on the windowsill above the sink, she lied and told him it was for one of their sons, for Carlitos' science project. Ricardo was a simple man, and she knew he would never understand why she would want to bring dried leaves to a woman down the street who some were convinced could see the future. It was better that nothing be said about that at all. Rosa Blanco kept very few things from her husband, but she knew he would not approve of this. She knew it wasn't the leaves that he would disapprove of or the fact the old woman could see the future, it was the need some had to seek out the old woman in order to see their own futures. Ricardo would never understand that.

When Rosa Blanco returned to the old woman's house, the door opened just before she knocked.

"You are right on time."

"I am?" Rosa Blanco replied.

"Yes. This is when I expected you to come."

"Now, today, this very day?"

"Yes, this very afternoon."

"But . . ."

"Did you bring me the leaves?"

"Yes, I . . ."

"Give them to me."

Rosa Blanco handed the leaves over to the old woman, who took them from her as if they were precious metals or jewels. She held them flatly against her palms, her two hands open and facing upward, as if she were carrying a gift to a god. She walked slowly into the sunroom in the back of the small house so as not to disturb the leaves in her hands, the sunroom adjoining the small kitchen. She didn't so much as slow down when they passed the living room. In the sunroom, she set the leaves down on the table and asked Rosa Blanco to come sit with her.

Nothing was asked of the old woman. Rosa Blanco never had a chance to ask anything. The old woman sat, stared at the leaves, bent her face down to them and sniffed them, then sat straight up and, without looking, clutched the leaves in her hands and crumbled them into scraps and shreds, the leaves making an uncomfortable crunching, almost crackling noise. The old woman closed her eyes and concentrated deeply as she moved her hands over the crumbled leaves. It was clear to Rosa Blanco that Flora Diaz had performed this action countless times in her life.

"You are married," Flora said.

"Yes!"

"You have two sons. You were to have had a girl but she died before you could deliver her."

"Yes. How did you . . ."

"Silence. I'm not asking."

Rosa Blanco was surprised. The old woman suddenly sounded younger, as if in the act of crushing the leaves she had grown younger, her voice now more vibrant and powerful.

"Your husband works for the mechanic. His father and your father are like brothers. You have known each other your entire lives, have been like family from before you were married."

Rosa Blanco was afraid to say anything now, but she wanted to say yes to everything the old woman was saying. But she dared not speak, dared not say anything that might upset the old woman and stop her from doing what she was doing.

"Your husband is . . . Your . . . Your husband is a follower. He is about to find someone who can master the air, someone who can be seen but is unseen by most. Your husband is going to pick up and follow him because it will seem as if he has answers. There will be no answers. There will be nothing but time passing and air. And you will hurt. You will feel pain inside your chest. You will hurt each day you look at your sons because in them you will see your husband. And your husband will be gone. And your husband will never return."

Rosa Blanco wanted to scream, wanted to cry, but she did nothing like that. She thanked the old woman politely and rose. "But I am not finished . . ." the old woman had started to say, but Rosa Blanco was already walking quickly back through the house toward the front door. It would be several years before she set foot inside Flora Diaz's house again. Years would pass before she ever spoke again to the old woman.

Rosa Blanco's husband did, as you know, leave. Trust me, I know far more about that than anything else in this story. One night, a few months after she had visited Flora Diaz, Ricardo did not come home from his evening job at LAX airport. Weeks passed, months passed and, eventually, years passed. He never came home, never called, and still Rosa Blanco expected him to come back. There were times when she absolutely believed he would come walking through the door. She imagined she would hear a noise at the door, then the key in the lock, and then the door opening. She imagined he would walk in carrying gifts for her and the boys, that they would laugh together, that he would tell her stories of faraway places and how he had left only to be able to return like this, return with gifts and money and and and . . . But Ricardo never came back, and the boys grew taller. The boys looked more and more like their father as each year passed. And Rosa Blanco had long ago stopped trying to explain to them where their father was. She stopped talking about him altogether. And then one day, in the grocery store, at the checkout counter while talking to Carmen Jiménez, Rosa Blanco saw the old woman again.

"I thought she was gone," Rosa said.

"Who, old Flora?"

"Yes, I thought she had moved away."

"Girl, you crazy?" responded Carmen Jiménez. "She always around."

"But I have not seen her."

"Well you need glasses, Rosa. Because she always around."

"I want to talk to you about something, but not here. Stop by my house on your way home tonight."

Rosa Blanco was more afraid of Flora Diaz then than she had been years earlier when she had visited her the second time, but she didn't understand what that sensation was. She had been afraid of so many things in her life, but not in this way. She remembered the old woman that day, the way she had said Ricardo would follow someone who could master the air. She wondered if that meant he had gotten into a fight and fallen over a cliff side or something. She wondered if the old woman knew where Ricardo was but had been hiding so as not to have to tell her. She wanted to talk to Flora Diaz, but she was worried about what the old woman might tell her. And she was envious of Carmen, Carmen who always got good news from the old woman, wonderful and brilliant news.

When Rosa Blanco got home from the store, the boys were nowhere to be found. More and more they, too, were missing. They would stumble in reeking of cigarette smoke, sometimes marijuana. She knew that sometimes they were drunk. And her little Carlitos, well, he wasn't so little anymore. She sat in the kitchen and waited. She checked on the soup in the big pot, chopped up some cilantro and onions and stirred them in, chopped up a tomato and stirred it in, poured in a cup of rice and left it all to simmer. She caught her own reflection in the kettle and decided she looked old, haggard, and witch-like. She waited on the soup, waited on her boys, and waited for Carmen Jiménez to stop by on her walk home from the store. When Carmen walked by the kitchen window, Rosa Blanco stood up and moved toward the back door. She pulled the door open and pushed the screen door out as an invitation. Carmen came in chattering as always. She told her about an old man propositioning her right at the checkout stand in front of others and how she thought the new clerk was an idiot. Finally, Rosa Blanco broke in:

"I never told you, but I went to see Flora Diaz years ago."

"Then why you so crazy today when she came into the store?"

"She told me Ricardo was going to leave . . ."

"Oh, Rosa. You never told me."

"I took her the leaves from a plant in the backyard. I did as she wanted me to do, dried them and made sure they were brittle."

"And that is all she said? That he was going to leave?"

"I wish I could say I couldn't remember, but I do. It was strange, the things she said."

"Well, she is a strange old woman, that Flora."

"She said Ricardo would leave to follow a master of the air. I think he may have fallen over a cliff or a ledge or something. I am worried. I think he may have gotten into a fight."

"Rosa, you can't worry about that man. Shit, you shouldn't worry about him at all. He just left. You think he worried about you? That man . . ."

"I am just worried because it makes no sense."

"Life never makes sense, girl. You got to know by know. It makes no sense."

"When I saw her today, I couldn't believe it. I have not seen her since the day she told me that terrible thing."

"But Rosa, that is impossible! She lives less than half a block away from you. You must have seen her. I see her all the time."

"But you work in the grocery store."

"But I see her all over the place. Rosa, it is impossible you haven't seen her all this time."

Rosa Blanco didn't know what to say. She knew she had not seen the old woman. She had actually believed the old woman had moved away, or was sick, or had died. She was 100% certain she had not seen her for ages, had not laid eyes on her until earlier that day in the grocery store. And this, in Rosa Blanco's head, had to be a sign. It had to be a sign. Maybe it was Flora Diaz's way of letting her know it was time to talk again. Maybe it was time for Ricardo to come home.

"It is just that I think maybe she came there today so that I would see her."

"Rosa, girl, you crazy. You know that? You crazy. If you want to talk to Flora Diaz, go talk to her."

"But why haven't I seen her since that day when . . ."

"You had to have seen her, Rosa. You had to have seen her."

"Maybe I will go talk to her. It is just that . . ."

"Look, girl, I have to get going. I got to get home and start dinner."

"Will you come with me to see Flora Diaz?"

"I don't think that is the right thing, Rosa. She don't do groups. She don't like to feel all ganged up on."

"But it is just that I think it would be better."

"Rosa, some things in life you just got to do on your own. You know?"

Carmen Jiménez didn't say much more because she was practically in the yard by the time Rosa Blanco tried to say another word. She was in the yard and then walking past the house and then on the sidewalk walking home. Rosa Blanco hadn't even gotten up from the table. She heard the front door and the boys arguing about something. It seemed they were always arguing about something then. She called out to them that dinner was waiting, that they needed to do something about pruning the tree in the front yard. She had been asking them to trim back that straggly tree for almost two weeks, and they had ignored her time and time again.

When Rosa Blanco made it to Flora Diaz's house weeks later, she was prepared. She brought with her some leaves she had pulled from the unkempt small tree in the front yard, the one that desperately needed pruning. She had plucked them almost a week before and left them to dry out on the front steps. When she reached the front door of the old woman's house, the door opened. Flora Diaz looked no older than the day three years earlier when Rosa Blanco had last gone there. Flora stood in the doorway but did not move.

"Why are you here?"

"I brought you some leaves."

"You brought me some leaves? Why?"

"I need to know."

"You *need* to? No, you do not need to know. You *want* to know."

"My husband, what happened?"

"You left before I could finish telling you about your husband."

"I was frightened then, but now I am . . . I just . . . Please tell me."

"I cannot remember now. What I do remember is that you left before I could finish."

"But you must remember something."

"I threw away those leaves a week after you left. I had hoped you would return, but once I thought on it, I knew you would not return until now."

"But don't you remember anything?"

"I threw the leaves away."

"Nothing? You remember nothing?"

"You should have come back to see me then. You didn't. Why you didn't return, only you know that."

"I, I don't remember. But, I am begging you . . . You must tell me the rest . . ."

"I am not one to keep things like that."

"But you told me about the master of the air."

Flora Diaz stepped back and then turned, let Rosa Blanco enter her house. She shut the door and then walked to the sunroom. She said nothing as she walked. And Rosa Blanco noticed this time how bright the sunroom was, how the walls were painted yellow, how there were plants hanging in baskets and that the plants had purple leaves. She noticed how the table was pale wood, that it was unpainted, unvarnished, blonde almost, and yet it had not a single stain on it. In the corner of the room, she saw a small ficus in a large pot. She noticed the floor was white linoleum that also had not a single stain or scuff mark. It was as if Flora Diaz never walked much less lived in this room.

"You told me he followed a master of air. Does this mean he fell over a cliff?"

"I do not remember." The two women sat at the table. Flora Diaz stared out the window. Rosa Blanco stared at Flora Diaz.

"Please. I am truly sorry for leaving that day, but I need to know what happened."

"I promise you, I remember nothing about what those leaves gave up."

"But you were so . . ."

"I did not keep the leaves. I threw them away."

"Well, I have more leaves for you."

"But these will not reveal what those other leaves did."

"Then I can go get some crocus leaves from the yard and dry them and come back in a few days."

"But those will not be the crocus leaves I threw away. Don't you see? The leaves show only one thread. No set of leaves gives you a chance to see the same thread."

"Okay, but these leaves I have here, might they show you a similar thread?"

"It is unlikely. Where did you get these leaves?"

"From the tree in the front of my house. But they might show you something, right?"

"From the shak shak tree?"

"I don't know what kind of tree it is. I have no idea. It was there when we moved in."

"Where I am from, we call it the shak shak tree, the flamboyant tree. I have no idea, but I will try for you. I will call to these leaves, but these leaves will probably show a different thread."

"But you will use them?"

"I will look."

Again, she held the leaves in her upturned palms and stared at them for what seemed like an hour to Rosa Blanco. She crumbled them on to the table and bent toward them and inhaled. She sat up and then placed her hands over them. Her brow furrowed and then she closed her eyes. After a minute, she put her hands in her lap and sighed.

"You saw Ricardo, didn't you? You saw him."

"No. I did not see him."

"You are lying. You saw him. I could see the change in your face."

"It was a different thread. It was completely different."

"But it was related, right?"

"Yes."

"So why won't you tell me about him. Where is he? Is he okay? Do I need to call the police?"

"The thread is related but is not the same. I could not see your husband. These leaves show nothing of your husband."

"Then why won't you tell me what you saw?"

"I just think . . . I just think that sometimes it is best not to reveal what is seen in a thread."

"Please. I am begging you."

"It is just that it isn't a good thing."

"I don't care this time. I want to know the whole thing. I am not leaving this time. I need to know. I will not leave until you tell me the entire thing. Do you understand me?"

"Trust me, you do not want to know this."

"I do. I want to know, you terrible old woman, you terrible old *bruja*!"

Rosa Blanco could not believe her own mouth, could not believe what she had heard herself say. It was as if she were listening to someone else speaking, as if she were watching the whole thing on one of the *telenovelas*. She must have remembered Carmen in the kitchen, remembered her saying she was crazy. And there, for what may have been the first time in her life, Rosa Blanco likely believed she might well be going crazy. She wanted to know. She wanted the smug old woman to tell her the truth, to tell her what she had seen in the leaves.

"Fine. I will tell you."

"Thank you."

"In your yard. In your very yard, one of your lives will end another."

"What does that mean?"

"One part of you will end another part of you."

"I am going to hurt myself? Am I going to fall in my yard and break something?"

"One Ricardo will kill the other Ricardo." The old woman closed her eyes and spoke slowly, very slowly: "One son will kill the other son."

Rosa Blanco said nothing. She put her head down on the table, her forehead against the clean wood and cried like she had never cried. She sobbed and shook. She felt herself shaking and could not stop it. She felt as if she were gasping for air. And Flora Diaz? She stood up from the table, walked back through her house, picked up her small hand broom and went out on the front step to dust it off. She swished the small broom back and forth. She paused and looked the length of the street from right to left, looked up toward Rosa Blanco's yard. She had no idea what to do with Rosa Blanco. She had seen the future, but she had no idea what to do now to help this strange woman. Inside, the sobs were still sputtering out of Rosa. Flora Diaz stood on her tiny front porch. She crossed it two or three times like a pacing cat. She swished the broom back and forth, the rhythm of it a background noise for the sobbing woman still in the sunroom next to her kitchen. She watched two figures coming down the road, easier and easier to make out as they got closer. The Blanco boys. She watched them but pretended to be sweeping the front steps.

V. *Desaparecido*

People play games. They cannot help it. They play them long after they are age-appropriate. They play them because they play them. No one knows why. Haven't you seen old women playing cat's cradle or duck duck goose? Haven't you watched grown men playing dodge ball, tug-of-war, punch-the-target, and the penknife game? The ones where they shout out different kinds of dares and exact various punishments on each other? People play games, and the Blanco boys were no different.

"When are you coming home? The boys keep asking."

"Oh, I don't know. I need another month or so."

"Really? A whole month more?"

"At least a month, but maybe more."

"Do you have a good job? Will you send us some money?"

"No, bitch! Not a dime."

The boys laughed out loud. Pedro always made their father into a cursing and vulgar man, even though he had never heard his father curse or utter a bad word to their mother or anyone else when he still lived at home with them. I can tell you that long after Ricardo left his family he remained very much a man who never used vulgar language or casual profanities. Bad language, surprisingly, was something Ricardo carefully avoided. Not once in our time together did I hear him curse. But this was Pedro's version of his father, this man who called his wife "bitch." Carlitos always laughed. He couldn't help it. Pedro would laugh, and then he had to laugh, too. It was infectious.

"But we cannot make it much longer," Carlitos said without even trying to imitate his mother's voice in that instance.

"Well, that's too fucking bad. I have things to do, woman. Important things."

"But how will we . . ."

"Not another word, bitch. Not another word!"

The boys had tried when they were much younger to construct a telephone with two cans and string, the way they had seen kids do on a television show, but they had no string and used, instead, a wire hanger pried apart and stretched between them; they shoved the ends of the hanger into the small holes they had punctured in the Progresso cans with the points of small gardening sheers. They never so much as removed the labels from the cans. Within days of putting together their phone, they couldn't find the hanger. Despite a panicked search that could only be panicky for small kids, they never found it. It simply vanished. Sitting cross-legged and hunched over in the basement, the hanger had been missing for years, but they continued to place the cans to their ears and talk to each other out of habit, a strange reflex, sitting close together as if the wire hanger were still there stretched between them. They did this less than when they were younger, but they still found themselves, every so often, in the basement, playing phone call.

To call it a basement was a stretch. Crawlspace was a better word, this dark and dank space beneath the front porch was where phone call happened. The only light to be found there were the small diamond-shaped beams created by the latticework of wood long since painted white and extending from the lip of the porch down to the hard soil that couldn't even support weeds much less grass, the beams of light making little diamonds that wavered on the dark ground beneath them. Phone call could happen nowhere else. Such a thing would have been unthinkable to those boys. And that Sunday, like most other Sundays, the conversation that took place was between their mother and father. The conversation always took place between their mother and father, Rosa and Ricardo Blanco.

"Look woman, I needed space. I just fucking needed to get the hell out of that house."

"But Ricardo. I have fixed up the garage so you can have your own space. Your own, no one else's."

Pedro stopped, put the can down, and stared at Carlitos. He was surprised to hear Carlitos use their father's name. Usually, he would use "*Papi*" or "Great Vacancy" or "Chicken Head" or something else. That Carlitos used the name "Ricardo" bothered Pedro, bothered him enough to halt the game. It bothered him more than he could even explain to himself. It broke the "rules" of phone call. And phone call, like any other game, had rules. For one, their mother almost never said their father's name out loud. And secondly, Pedro was old enough to remember his father chastising him when he was small for using his name, his Christian name, instead of simply calling him *Papi*. Pedro continued staring at his brother with what many of us would call venom in his eyes.

Carlitos knew he had gone too far. He had disappointed Pedro before. But he was tired of playing the role of his mother in the conversation. He was always Rosa Blanco in this game, and it was difficult being his mother, though he knew he was every bit as anxious as she was, every bit as nervous, too. He wanted to be his father, Ricardo Blanco, whether or not he spoke the name on the phone. He wanted a life of excitement where the rules didn't matter or at least weren't enforced. It would be easier for him not to say his father's name if he got the chance to play his father in the game because folks don't talk about themselves in third person. It would then be Pedro's job to leave the name unsaid, to follow the rules.

In Church that morning, Rosa Blanco insisted her boys go to Confession, something Carlitos hated more than almost anything else. In this, he was very much like his father. In this, he was very much like most men. And like his father, he hated saying Confession more than standing in line for Holy Communion or the repeated kneeling-sitting-standing-kneeling throughout Mass. What Carlitos noted after years of study was the fact that the events of Mass followed so many rules. Everything had to be done in a certain way and in a certain order. It was like a very long and boring game. You can imagine how this could drive a young boy mad, that incessant need for rule and order.

Because there was only one priest at the Church, Carlitos knew, like everyone did, exactly who was behind the dark screen listening to him reveal his transgressions. Father Happy was in there, rolling his eyes or holding back a sigh. No one could remember Father Happy's real name. Good old Father Happy, who wasn't even old, whose attempts at Spanish made it all too clear he had learned it from a set of cassettes and not actual people. But the Church would never send an older priest here. Just like the many islands in the Caribbean, just like the poor towns dotting Mexico and Central America, the Ciudad Juarezes and the Managuas, the easy to ignore towns of southern California with their Spanish names were just other dying outposts of Spain. Holy Mother Church always sent the younger priests here, the ones without seniority, the ones who could endure brown people like us who lived in towns named after angels and saints. And Father Happy wasn't just young; he tried to act as if he were even younger than he actually was.

Carlitos guessed Father Happy was in his early thirties, but Father Happy wanted to talk to the young people as if he were twenty. When he spoke English, he tried to do so with a Spanish accent. But he got the accent wrong for the area. He would say, "How you doing, mang?" without any realization his accent sounded like a bad imitation of a *boricua* loan shark and not remotely like the Mexican-inflected English most spoke in the area. When he came close to using English the way Chicanos in the area did, he came off sounding like an actor playing a *vato* on a television movie special, a *vato* who everyone knew would be busted for selling dope and then incarcerated before the final credits. He would ask Carlitos if he listened to Snoop Dogg, or had he seen the new show on MTV. Father Happy was a pretty bad imitation of a twenty-year-old guy. And what twenty-year-old guy would be a priest anyway?

Carlitos lied that morning in the Confessional. He lied because he was tired and didn't want to think about his sins. So, as he often did, he made them up on the fly. We have all done this. All men do this. And though we don't like to think about it, even some women do this. Kneeling at the screened window in the dark cubicle, Father Happy's shadow shifting behind it, the first thing Carlitos could think to confess was about touching himself inappropriately and having impure thoughts. That was an easy sin to confess. What priest would doubt such a confession from a thirteen-year-old boy? But the reality was that Carlitos had not had impure thoughts, at least not that he could remember. And he had not touched himself in that way, at least not in the past week. The house was small, and he had little time to himself. The shower cubicle in the bathroom had no curtain, just a plexiglass door that, despite being opaque from calcium deposits, was easily seen through. There was always the chance Pedro would walk into the bathroom while he was showering, and had his brother caught him in the shower like that, Carlitos would never have heard the end of it. Despite the fact Pedro had taught Carlitos how to jack off, he would have taunted his little brother mercilessly.

But there in the Confessional, the sins Carlitos chose to confess got more and more outrageous and ended with him telling the priest how he had beaten his brother with a switch, beaten him until blood ran from his neck. As he told the priest this, his voice trembled like a practiced actor. The words stuttered from his mouth in what could only be called an Oscar-caliber performance. It was so good Carlitos practically convinced himself he had actually done this, beaten Pedro with a switch!

But what impressed Carlitos the most was the fact this confessed beating required thirty Hail Marys more than the simple admission of masturbation. And in the end, Carlitos only said eight Hail Marys and a single Our Father. He was thinking ahead. He knew that by skimping on the prayers he would have something to confess the following Sunday. And he couldn't wait to find out how many Hail Marys he would have to say for admitting he hadn't done the required amount of penance for the terrible sin of beating his brother with a switch. When he rose from kneeling, he had to work hard to erase the smirk from his face before he stepped from the dark little box into the alcove in the back of the Church, speckled as it was then by the light filtered through the stained glass, his upturned hands, as he walked slowly through the shifting colors, yellow then pink then a reddish hue.

Rosa Blanco called out to her sons, and they dropped the cans and crawled out from under the house. She was tired. Her voice was tired. It had that sound, the one that made them worry. Her voice and its tremulous quality often made them worry, even if they could not identify the feeling as worry to someone else. Neither of those boys could tell with any certainty whether or not the voice was genuine, put on, or put on for so long it had become a habit. But her voice made them nervous at times, made them worry even when they couldn't place a finger on exactly why. They found her in the kitchen with her head in her hands, sitting under the telephone. It hung there, that awkward yellow phone that made no attempt to match all of the avocado-green things in the kitchen. It did not ring. It just hung there on the wall, its slim body like the body of an exclamation point. She reminded them the tree in the front yard needed pruning, told them that it had become too straggly and terrible looking. She told them they needed to trim it back soon and that she wasn't going to ask them again. And Pedro watched Carlitos. He watched Carlitos' eyes and where they focused. He watched Carlitos staring at the phone.

The boys didn't prune the tree. Did you really expect them to do as their mother asked when she asked them? They were adolescent boys, and like most their age, their decision not to do something had less to do with shirking responsibility than it did a straight-out lack of focus. They went outside and stared at it, instead. It was, indeed, straggly and unkempt, this tree and its occasional red petals punctuating the shapeless branches with little points of red, a berry red almost like something from a Christmas card. Neither one of them really had any intention of trimming back the tree. The tree almost never seemed to grow. And yet, it became messy, its branches thin, almost like fingers, reaching out in all manner of different directions. Pedro sat on the sidewalk trying to think of ways to get cigarettes from the corner store several blocks away. Pedro was good at getting older guys to give him cigarettes on their way out of the store, could talk the cool talk and be "down" as he put it. Pedro always wanted to smoke. He liked it in a way Carlitos didn't. Smoking made Carlitos feel light-headed, almost dizzy. It made the muscles in his legs feel tingly and as if someone had stretched them.

Carlitos became aware then that he and Pedro were being watched. Like any other animal, he had become aware of eyes trained on him, tracking him. Somewhere deep in our genes, this protective instinct had been passed down over millennia. And despite the passage of so much time, this reflex, if you could call it that, still functioned. If anything, it is the living proof that human beings were not always the hunters, that the likely truth is that for ages we were, in fact, the hunted. Carlitos turned then, turned slowly at the neck, to look to the right of their own house. He turned his attention a few houses down the street to check the front porch of Flora Diaz's house. But this time, to his surprise, the hunter was not Flora Diaz sweeping her front steps while watching them. Instead, standing there that afternoon, was a man with skin as dark as their own, a man Carlitos was sure he had seen before. But before he could think further on it, on where he had seen this man, Carlitos realized Pedro was talking again, his voice more and more agitated.

"I can't wait to get the fuck out of here. This place sucks hole."

"But Pedro, you're sixteen . . ."

"Men get girls pregnant at sixteen!"

"Yeah, but how are you going to make money to live?"

"I can work in the fields somewhere. I can work in a store."

"The corner store?"

"No, shithead. In a store far away."

Carlitos knew Pedro was talking just to talk. So, he ignored him, which was something rare. Carlitos usually hung on every word his brother said. But all of this talk of leaving was just too strange. People in their town never seemed to leave. Except for their father. Their father left, something no one in their small *barrio* could understand, even if most of them wanted to leave as well. Carlitos sat there and let Pedro go on and on about leaving, about meeting lots of women, about how he would party and have fun, smoke endless amounts of weed. Carlitos knew it was all talk. Pedro didn't know how to do anything except skip school, smoke cigarettes, and mouth off. Carlitos tried, as hard as he could, to remember when Pedro had become that way. When they were younger, Pedro was always quiet. Their mother had worried Pedro had a speech impediment or some kind of mental problem. The school had put him in a special class, but everyone knew that such a class was anything but special. And what Carlitos knew was that Pedro hated the class, even though he never actually admitted that. Even at that young age, Carlitos knew he did not ever want to be in such a class. That class was nothing but a jail cell for seven hours each weekday.

"Let's go back to phone call."

"Nah. I don't want to go down there."

"You are such a loser sometimes. You know that?"

"Yeah, I know."

"Loser with a capital fucking 'L.'"

"Yeah. Capital 'L.'"

Carlitos again felt as if he and his brother were being watched, but when he turned to look at the front of Flora Diaz's house, the man he had seen earlier was gone, replaced now by Flora Diaz herself, Flora Diaz watching them while sweeping her steps with her small handbroom. The man had neither walked away from the house down toward the corner store or up toward them. No car had driven off. There had been no sound of a screen door creaking open or slamming shut. All that was there now was Flora Diaz swishing her small broom and what Carlitos knew was certainly a look of displeasure on her face. She always had a look of annoyance on her face when she looked at them.

"Bless me, Father, for I have sinned." It had been two weeks since Carlitos had done the lesser penance, but he had forgotten to confess it the previous Sunday. He had confessed, instead, to stealing Twinkies from the corner store, to ignoring his mother, and, the old standby, touching himself. He had not stolen Twinkies, but he had jacked off, and he couldn't remember if he had ignored his mother or not. So, now, he was excited to confess he had not said all of his Hail Marys or his Our Fathers. This was a true confession, even if it had not happened that week.

As always, Carlitos could make out the shape of Father Happy's head even though all he could see was the shadow of it against the screen. Father Happy appeared to be desperately trying to hold still, or maybe he was leaning against his hand with his elbow on a desk or ledge of some kind. Father Happy sighed and tapped at the screen, his one way of telling a sinner to hurry up, spill it, confess.

"It has been one week since my last confession."

"Yes, my son, go on . . ." Father Happy sighed.

"You see, Father, I didn't do my entire penance last week. I was tired, so I didn't say all of the Hail Marys or Our Fathers."

"But were you sorry for your sins? Did you want to say the prayers?"

"Yes, but I was tired."

Carlitos knew he was lying, but the lying made him even more excited. He knew he hadn't been tired. He knew he had skimped on his penance because he wanted to confess that later, wanted to test the grand schema of the Sacrament of Confession with all of its rules for penance. But there, in the dark and musty Confessional, the ripeness of the last confessor's armpits still lingering in the closed box's air, this new lie took on a greater importance. Yes, he had been so tired, so overworked. He went on and on, the dim light in the priest's box staining the screen in front of him with Father Happy's awkward shadow, his neck always appearing longer in shadow, like a small giraffe, like a minor monster of some kind you find in a cartoon.

"God understands how tired we become. But he also knows when we are truly sorry. So, for taking food from the store, you should say ten Hail Marys. For your inappropriate acts, fifteen Hail Marys and an Our Father."

"But I haven't even confessed to stealing or touching myself yet! How can you give me penances when I haven't even confessed these things?"

"Did you not steal from the store this week? Did you not touch yourself?"

"Well, yeah, I did, Father. I stole a comic book from the corner store on Thursday. And well, I jacked off until I shot my load all over the bathroom tile. I did it several times this week to see how far I could shoot." Carlitos watched Father Happy's shadow as he said this, waited to see if there would be a change in his demeanor because of the slightly more vulgar way he described his inappropriate acts. But there was no change, just another sigh from Father Happy.

"Yeah, each time I came, each time I shot my load, it felt great, Father."

"Yes, this is the problem with sin, my son."

"But what about my being tired? My not saying the prayers?"

"God and His Holy Church forgive you, my tired son."

"Yes, but how many Hail Marys?"

"You wanted to say them, so your heart was true. You need not give penance for having a true heart."

"Are you serious, Father?"

"Yes, my son. God's gift is the gift of understanding."

Carlitos was outraged. No prayers for an incomplete penance? An incomplete penance for supposedly striking his brother with a switch? He expected Father Happy to give him the largest penance he had ever received. He wanted fifty Hail Marys. He expected some Our Fathers thrown in and even a full rosary or two at the Stations of the Cross. Father Happy had confused him. The scale of penance seemed misaligned. The Sacrament of Confession seemed misaligned. How was this possible? But all Carlitos could say was a brief "Thank you, Father" and then promised to try harder in the coming week to avoid sin.

The overcast sky outside cast only a dim light through the stained glass that morning and, as Carlitos stepped from the Confessional, there were no pink or yellow hues on the hardwood floors polished to perfection. As he walked, he turned his palms up and saw only red. It was as if even the light outside had decided to cease following the rules. Even Carlitos' white shirt appeared reddened from the light slowly passing through the stained glass above him, the lighter colors somehow incapable of reaching very far in that poor light. When he looked up, Rosa Blanco was standing in the corner waiting for him, her face dim and sad as always. Carlitos could not recall his mother's face any other way, could not remember her smiling; it had been so long.

Pedro stayed home that Sunday. At least that is what I remember when I try to recall the whole thing the way it was told to me. I admit that there are some discrepancies about the entire thing when I think about it too carefully. But that is beside the point. The way I remember it, Pedro stayed home that Sunday morning because he had announced he was sick and kept coughing whenever his mother was nearby. Rosa Blanco supposedly told him to stay in bed, drink lots of water, and to say some prayers. But when Carlitos and his mother got home, Pedro was not there. He showed up an hour or so later with a story of how he had prayed and then felt better within a half an hour. All that Rosa Blanco said in response was "God is powerful," before retreating to the kitchen.

"That one stupid white boy that lives at the end of the block gave me four cigarettes. We should go smoke under the house."

"I don't feel like it."

"Bitch, you such a baby."

"Yeah."

"Don't tell me, 'yeah.' Just come down there with me."

Carlitos went down into the crawl space with Pedro. He always expected to find a demon down there or, at a minimum, a large rat. He hated that space, but he found it more and more difficult to disobey his brother. He didn't plan on smoking but went just so his brother didn't have to go down there alone. Of course he ended up smoking a cigarette. And, of course, they ended up playing phone call. And again, Carlitos let his father's name slip.

"Shit, man. You don't understand this game. You keep forgetting the rules."

"I'm sorry, Pedro. I didn't mean to . . ."

"You never gonna do that again."

"I really didn't mean to . . ."

"I don't fucking care!"

Once again, their mother's voice could be heard calling their names. Her voice was strained and sad, almost close to breaking. And again, as she had done many times over the previous weeks, she was calling them to prune the tree in the front yard. They dropped the cans. They crawled out from under the house, the smell of cigarette smoke in their clothes, their hair, the smoke itself still winding its way out from under the house through the lattice-work that wrapped around the underside of the porch. Pedro and Carlitos had no idea what kind of tree it was standing in their front yard, just that it was the biggest tree they had and that it was "a mess." It wasn't even very big, just slightly taller than Pedro, but it was still the largest tree in the yard.

Carlitos called it a eucalyptus tree, but neither of them really knew if it was or not. Carlitos had seen the name "eucalyptus" in a book at school. Months later, he had seen an article in the newspaper about how the eucalyptus trees were dying off, how they had killed off much of the natural vegetation in the areas they were planted, their leaves making the soil around them acidic and poisonous to most plants. Very little grew in the front yard, so Carlitos took this as proof the tree was a eucalyptus. The article seemed to be rejoicing in the fact these trees were slowly disappearing from the California flora. But the only Flora that Carlitos knew was the old woman down the street who swept her front steps every afternoon, usually at 2:00 p.m. It was always hotter than hell at that time of day. Crazy old whore, Pedro called her, among other things.

The small tree, without even a remote idea of shape, thrust its finger-like, thin branches in all different directions, but it was not a eucalyptus tree. That much I know. That much I can tell you. At times, that stunted tree surprised itself with a shock of small blood-red flowers. At other times, the telltale elongated pods filled with seeds hung from it. It had no business being in southern California. It made its way there, like so many other things, because of the Spaniards. And its inability to grow as large as the ones found elsewhere in the world was likely a result of the terrible soil in the area. To be honest, I have never seen one in that part of the world. It was most definitely not a eucalyptus tree. It was a royal poinciana, the same one called the Flamboyant Tree by the *Conquistadores*, what we in the islands called the shak shak tree.

Pedro had pruned it before, but Carlitos had been too young to help then. Carlitos was worried about what to do, worried he might cut too much of the tree back and then end up killing it. He remembered hearing one of the men who worked in the fields talk about this, how sometimes *los gringos* pruned trees so much they just died. When Carlitos told Pedro this, he laughed and said something about white people being stupid. Pedro handed Carlitos the large instrument that looked like giant thickened scissors and laughed: "You Mexican too, boy." Carlitos started cutting the straggly branches. They snapped with each click of the instrument locking. It not only looked like scissors but worked like scissors as well. Pedro was singing something about shooting *gringos*. The song made no sense to Carlitos, but the clicking as he snapped the straggly branches set up a kind of drumbeat for Pedro. Carlitos could see Flora out on her front step staring at them. But she wouldn't come out onto the sidewalk or her driveway. It was too late in the day for that. It was shadow time, the light throwing lines across the yards, the sun within an hour or so of setting.

"It's been more than three years now."

"Yeah. So?"

"He's never coming back, is he?"

"That man dead. He as dead as deadly."

"But suppose he's not dead."

"So? Suppose he's not. What does it matter?"

"Then he might come back."

"Bitch, he never coming home. ¡*Él ha desaparecido*!"

Carlitos stopped the trimming and stood there with a blank look on his face. He had never heard Pedro speak Spanish to him in this way. Pedro had never used more than, say, a single word for emphasis: *vato*, *puta*, *mierda*, *cabrón*. He used them as a kind of punctuation at the end of sentences, sentences usually addressing Carlitos or the stupid *gringo* boy at the end of the street. But an entire sentence? In Spanish? He had never heard such a thing from his brother. And why he understood it, not just what the words meant but what they really meant, was unexplainable even to his own mind.

Carlitos cut the largest branch last. He held it in his hand. He felt the weight of it. He looked at Pedro. He looked at the back of Pedro's head. Carlitos gripped the branch. *Desaparecido*. The word was lodged in his head. He gripped the branch. He gripped it tighter, felt the bark pressing into the lines of his palm. A splinter of the bark pierced his skin. But he didn't let go. He gripped it with his left hand, the one the old nun at the grade school called "sinister." *Desaparecido*. He gripped it until tears welled in his eyes. There was the viscous sensation of blood in his palm and the sun, now setting, heating his face. There was his brother's neck, the back of it, brown and dirty, dirty and terrible. He gripped the branch. He gripped it as his hands went numb and his feet went numb. *Desaparecido*. He felt the weight of it. The branch, in his hand, was like a switch. He lifted his arm. He stared at Pedro's dirty neck. He felt the blood in his palm, felt it sticky against the branch, and the branch was like a switch. As he stared at the back of Pedro's neck, he wondered how many prayers he would have to say as penance for intentionally striking his brother. The branch was like a switch. It came down with incredible force.

VI. Between Men

You never know you want to live until someone tells you that you will die. For four years, Leenck had worked from home processing accounts for an investment firm. Leenck was, suffice it to say, painfully aware that he was dying. He had already gone to the bank and withdrawn all of his savings: at the counter waiting for this manager or that supervisor to sign this or that form, the teller had looked at him that morning as if she, too, knew he was dying. It was as if everyone stared at him. When Leenck arrived at his home, he telephoned his lawyer and told him to find a house for him to rent in Santa Monica, a small house near the beach, a house where no one would notice him. And within a few days, Leenck packed some of his clothes in a duffle bag and drove to the new place. It was that simple. He had no family in the U.S. His family had written him off for dead ages ago. He had no one who would notice him missing. His co-workers didn't even know what he looked like.

Leenck had no intention of getting to know Santa Monica. What he knew of it he knew by driving through it on his way to the new house, described in the real estate ad as a charming bungalow. It is always amazing the lies these ads can tell. One bedroom and one bathroom, a living room, a small kitchen, a patio and a strangely large yard, and still the new place seemed enormous to him, larger than he felt he deserved. The house came partially furnished. It had no table and chairs in the kitchen, and there was no dining area. The same linoleum covered the floors in both the kitchen and the living room. It was yellow, though it was easy to tell it had once been off-white. If one wanted to eat, such a thing would have to be done standing in the kitchen or sitting on the couch with the coffee table functioning as dining table. But there was a bed, a couch, said coffee table, and a plastic lounge chair in the backyard. There were overhead lights but no lamps, and Leenck had no intention of remedying that fact.

The beach was exactly an eight-minute walk away. And despite wanting to stay locked up inside the house, Leenck found himself walking down to the beach twice a day. It became a habit for him, a kind of pilgrimage. It was always the same. He would walk down his street, make a left-hand turn, and walk over the pedestrian bridge to the beach. Sometimes, he would walk on the pier, but mostly he just walked or stood on the sand.

Orange juice and sparkling wine: what more could one desire for breakfast? Each morning, Leenck drank a cup of instant coffee and then filled a tumbler with ice followed by a quarter glass of orange juice and the remaining three quarters of the glass with sparkling wine. The walk to the beach then followed. On some days, he would even forego the coffee. There were times when he would stay at the beach for hours. On other occasions, he would walk around for fifteen minutes and then walk home. He saw some of the same people at the beach almost daily. There was the old man who always wore pastel blues and pinks and sat on the rotting bench eating a bagel each morning. He was a man of few expressions. There was glum and glummer with only a mild change in his face as he ate the bagel. And there was the Chinese woman who did stretches and quick jabbing movements with her hands, jabbing at the air as if at birds only she could see, birds attacking her. There was the homeless man who wandered aimlessly muttering something about cats and cleanliness. There was the young woman briskly walking her small dog, a dog that always appeared better groomed than she did, at least four pink or red ribbons in its fur as if the mane on its head were in fact a hairstyle. The sun would be far behind them all, on the other side of the city. There would be light in the sky, but no sun. The sand would be a filthy grey dotted with trash, but at least the trash changed daily. The ocean would be there with its insistent noise and smell. At least there was this one constant. Leenck knew what he would find at the beach. He knew what each day brought. And each morning, on his walk, he wondered if his final day had come, if that very day was the one.

Some people, when faced with death, find themselves possessed with an undeniable urge to do things, to do everything they had ever wanted to do but had never found the time. They travel to distant lands. They jump off of bridges into murky water. They rappel down cliffs, fly in helicopters, dive in shark-infested waters, venture out on walking safaris in the bush hoping to hear the lion's unmistakable grumbling roar. They live and live dangerously because they know they are about to die. But Leenck was not one of those people. Honestly, neither am I. Leenck wanted to die privately. He was absolutely certain about this. He wanted to die alone. He wanted to disappear the way an actor playing the Buddha might in an old movie. It has taken me a long time, but I actually admire this about Leenck when I think of him now. But back then, I did not understand any of it.

"Hey man. You okay?" I said to Leenck. I could tell he had almost no idea what I had said to him. He turned around and stared at me with that odd expression on his face to which I would, over time, become quite accustomed. "I've seen you out here before. Man, you almost walked into that garbage can."

"Oh. Sorry. I was just thinking. Sorry."

"No problem, man. I do that sometimes, too. I'm Diego. Diego."

"Hi Diego, Diego."

Leenck was always amazed at the way Americans could just strike up conversations, how they always seemed to want to talk. Leenck believed that silence bothered Americans. And yet, I was the first person who had spoken to him at the beach. Leenck mumbled a few more things and said he had to get going. On the way home, Leenck must have wondered why I had talked to him. Later, he told me how once home, he had gone out on the patio, sat in his single lounge chair and fallen asleep. When he woke up, it was already late afternoon, time to return to the beach. On the walk to the beach then, Leenck noticed the creamsicle-colored blooms of the hibiscus in various yards. He wondered why anyone would plant such hideous plants with their gaudy display intermittently disturbing the hedges. He could hear the crackling of the telephone wires overhead once he made the turn toward the beach, knew that the humidity must have been fairly high that afternoon. Slowly, he found himself filled with anxiety that I would still be there at the beach. He was worried that maybe even someone else might talk to him. And so he stopped, turned around, and walked back to the house. Do I trust the story? Do I trust the way he recalled things? Not really. You know I don't trust the way many of these things are recalled. But memory is always like this. I don't pretend it can be any other way. I stopped pretending a long time ago.

*

"When did the pain start? What did you first notice?"

"I fell off of my bike a few weeks ago, and ever since then I have been sore."

"Where are you sore?"

"Here." Leenck pointed to his left side just where he felt the last of his rib bones, just under the skin.

"Did you take anything for it?"

"I took some Advil, some ibuprofen, and it helped a little. But I think I may have broken a rib."

"Well, we will take a look. But this doesn't sound like a broken rib. Sounds as if you bruised a muscle there." The doctor emphasized the word "bruised" as if Leenck might not have noticed the word otherwise. The doctor had a way of emphasizing words that made Leenck feel as if the doctor believed he were a complete idiot.

Leenck did not like doctors. In the old country, in the town where he grew up, there were no doctors. There was the old woman who was the teacher. She knew how to help people. She would touch you and tell you things about what hurt you. But these American doctors, they barely ever touched you. And when they did, they wore gloves as if they were handling raw meat. Doctor Peterson was probably a nice man, but to Leenck he was distant and calculating. He said little besides asking his various questions and, honestly, Leenck had only seen him once or twice. Despite his distrust, Leenck always did what the doctor said. He took the pills three times a day. Even when they made him feel sick to his stomach, he took them. He tried taking them with milk or when he ate something, but it didn't really help. Nothing he did to make taking the pills more bearable worked. He took the pills for two weeks, and they didn't help in the slightest. They only gave him a dry mouth and a sometimes-dizzy feeling in his head, as if he had had one too many drinks.

When Leenck returned to the clinic, the doctor seemed surprised that the pills hadn't worked. He sent Leenck for a CT Scan. Leenck sat in the waiting room outside the radiology department. And then he sat in a smaller waiting room inside. And then a nurse took him into the room with the giant donut-shaped scanner, placed a needle in his arm and had him lie down on the table, the room smelling a little like burning rubber. Above his head, he could see a red light on the top of the large ring that encircled the table. The table inched though the ring and then slid back out, the light sometimes green and sometimes red. And then, he felt the liquid tingle rushing through the needle and into his arm, and then he felt the table inching through the giant donut a little more. Ten minutes later, a young man told Leenck his spleen was very large and that he needed to call Doctor Peterson immediately.

For Leenck, that was not the beginning but the end. He called Doctor Peterson. He did more tests, had blood drawn, suffered through seeing a woman doctor, an oncologist, who rammed a large bore needle into his hip and pulled bloody fluid out into a syringe. He was warned of the pain but felt nothing. He was thirty-six years old, and he was dying. This is all he could remember about the woman doctor. Most of the time, he couldn't even remember her name.

*

Leenck hated the grocery store. There were just too many people darting around grabbing things and throwing them in carts: too many people talking to themselves about what they needed to pick up, how many, what size, etc. It irritated him to see people like this. It irritated him when people spoke to themselves out loud. He felt it was a weakness of some type, an indication of a feeble mind. He wanted to order groceries and have them delivered, but that would have meant having to set up phone service. And this was unthinkable to Leenck. Phone service, connection: what was the point? But he needed orange juice and more sparkling wine. He knew exactly where they were in the grocery store. He bought the most expensive orange juice and the least expensive sparkling wine. As Leenck walked down the aisle toward the produce section where the more expensive orange juices were shelved in a refrigerator, he saw me. Leenck knew that I also saw him, and you could practically see the gears turning in his head, see him thinking about how he might turn without making an incident. But it was too late. And I was quite intent on talking to him.

"Hey, you the guy from the beach. We talked. I'm Diego."

Leenck knew exactly who I was. In fact, I was the only person Leenck had seen who had dared to disturb him. "I don't think you ever told me your name," I said.

"Leenck."

"Is that Scandinavian?"

"You know, I am not really sure. My parents weren't Scandinavian. But they aren't around for me to ask them."

Leenck had both told the truth and lied in the same breath. As I discovered much later, his parents were in the old country, in Spain, the very same country that sent its people to infiltrate the far reaches of the globe from the Caribbean to the Americas to the Pacific itself, Balboa disassembling his ships on the shores of Panama in the Gulf of Mexico and then reassembling them on the opposite Pacific shore. Imagine that. Balboa used Panama to cross from the Gulf to the Pacific long before the Canal was even built there. But I am getting distracted. Suffice it to say that Leenck's parents were very much alive despite the fact Leenck made it sound then as if they were dead.

"Oh, sorry about that. My mother died when I was young," I said, "and, well, my father and I aren't really on speaking terms."

Leenck was trying to walk away now, but I followed. I continued telling him about my own family, how I had lived in the U.S. for a long time as well.

"You are not American?" Leenck asked.

"Oh no." I laughed. "I grew up on a small island in the Caribbean. My father's family is originally from Spain. My mother's family was Spanish and Indian."

"But you don't have much of an accent? I don't hear an accent when you speak English."

"You don't have an accent either . . ."

When Leenck reached the checkout and became aware that all he had was the sparkling wine and the orange juice, he grabbed a *TV Guide* and threw it on the belt along with the beverages. But Leenck had no television. I knew this. When he paid for his items, he nodded at me.

"Good talking with you, man," I said. "Maybe we'll run into each other again?"

"Yeah. Maybe. Yeah." Leenck was already worried he would see me again. It is funny how one can tell these things. I have always been able to tell a lot from people's expressions, usually much more than from what they actually say.

At home, Leenck fixed himself a tumbler of mimosa. He drank it all in one sitting and fixed himself another to sip while sitting in the backyard. The grass was withering in various places, but lush and green in others. The yard looked like a patchwork of greens and decay. The fence was unpainted on the side he could see. From outside his yard, the fence was white, almost pristine. But inside the yard, it was an unstained and unpainted fence that looked like it was rotting. The water from the sprinklers had given the fence a reddish rusty complexion. Did Leenck think about his parents? Did he speak to himself? I can almost imagine him saying: "No, they are not Scandinavian. They are most certainly not Scandinavian." I can imagine him saying a lot of things.

*

"You have a leukemia. This is a cancer of your white blood cells."

"How do we get rid of it?"

"Well, we can try to control it with chemotherapy . . ."

"What?"

"Chemotherapy. Drugs that will kill off some of your cancer cells."

"But you said control it. You cannot get rid of it?"

"No, this is a chronic leukemia. We cannot cure it."

"So, I'm going to die of this."

"Well some people live a very long time with this."

"What is a long time? What does this mean for me now?"

"Right now, we just need to focus on the diagnosis and getting started with chemotherapy."

"But . . . But, this is . . ."

"But nothing. We need to get started because your spleen is filled with cancer cells."

"I just need some time to think about this."

"We need to get started. You don't have a lot of time to think about this. . . ."

*

On that fateful day I remember well, Leenck woke to find himself scratching the scar he had on his left thigh. It had been a long time since he thought about this scar or how he got it. And it seemed as if it were all a dream, the way he had tried to impress his father by tying a wire around his thigh to show how far up a tree limb one should tie it off before cutting it. But it wasn't a dream, and the scar reminded him of that, reminded him of the old country and the simple way of life in which he had been raised. To Leenck, he had not been raised in a cult in Spain but just raised differently. And he wondered if his parents were still alive, though he knew they were because people in his family lived into their 90s if they were needed in the town. Yes, they were alive. They had to be. He could see them doing their everyday routines when he closed his eyes.

Leenck got up and went into the kitchen and made some instant coffee. He drank it quickly and made himself a mimosa. He took the drink out on to his backyard patio and sat there in his boxer shorts. The fence was definitely rotting. He swore he could almost smell the wood rotting. He got up from his lone chair and started walking around the backyard barefoot, around and around in circles. And when he got tired, he stopped and took off his boxer shorts, threw them on the ground, and stood there naked sipping mimosa from his tumbler, the sunlight warming his entire body. He stretched his arms and back. He slowly inspected the rotting and hideous fence. He walked over to it and started walking alongside it, slowly circling the yard. Along the eastern edge of the yard, he noticed one of the boards in the fence was loose and hanging at a slight angle.

He probably had no idea why he wanted to look through the space opened in the fence. Call it a childish curiosity, the kind we all know far too well. Leenck lowered himself on one knee and looked through the crack into his next-door-neighbor's yard. Lying on a towel on the grass in a pair of tight square swimming trunks was none other than me. Didn't you see this coming? I lived next door. Leenck bolted upright, ran over to his boxers and picked them up before running into his house and closing the sliding glass door behind him. He leaned against the glass door and downed the rest of his mimosa. He put his boxer shorts back on. He made himself another mimosa. That man from the beach, from the grocery store, Diego: I lived next door. To Leenck, this was just not possible. To Leenck, this was a terrible joke. But these things are never jokes, are they?

*

"This is Sheila from the Cancer Care Center calling for Leenck Woods. Please call us when you get this message. The doctor feels it is very important for you to come in for your treatments. We have left several messages for you, and the doctor is concerned. Please, if you have any questions or concerns about your treatments, please call us so you can speak to one of our nurses."

This was the last message Leenck heard on his answering machine before he left Los Angeles. When he recounted it to me, he always did so laughing. He had screened his calls for several days after he attended his chemotherapy training session. Poison. He believed they wanted to poison him. Not in the nefarious way they do in a movie, all plotting and scheming and then the fatal scene with a woman, always a woman, standing over someone. No, not like that, but he knew that chemotherapy was merely poison. He wasn't going to do it. He couldn't get himself to do it. He had decided to die. He had already gotten the house to rent in Santa Monica. He had already sold off all of his stocks and bonds and withdrawn all of his money from his various accounts. As he walked out the front door that day in Los Angeles, Leenck said out loud: "This is Leenck from the Office of the Dying. I feel it is very important for me to die, and I am therefore refusing chemotherapy." In other versions of this moment, he would add that he stopped and thought about what he said. "Hmmm. Maybe I should phrase it differently . . . This is Señor Bosque, Mr. Woods, Leenck. I have opted not to receive the treatment." Regardless of which version he recounted, after speaking to himself out loud, he always closed the door behind him. The power would be turned off that afternoon. He had no intention of ever calling the Cancer Care Center with its quiet shades of paint in the various rooms, the large glass windows looking out on exquisitely manicured gardens, its soft music piped into almost every corner of the place. He never did.

*

"You live next door to me."

"Yeah."

"Is that why you talked to me here that morning?"

"No man, I talked to you because you looked down and you almost walked into a garbage can."

"But you knew I lived next door to you."

"Yeah, I saw when you moved in. You didn't bring much with you."

Leenck looked down the beach beyond me and beyond the bench on which I was sitting. Some children were throwing a Frisbee and yelling "Fuck!" every time one of them didn't catch it.

"Why didn't you say anything?"

"About what? About living next door?"

"Yes, why didn't you . . ."

"Look man, when I first met you, you didn't seem to want to talk. You practically ran away."

Leenck turned and started walking away. In the distance, we heard, once again, "Fuck!"

"What is up with you, man? Is it a bad thing that I live next door?" I yelled as Leenck was already a good ten feet away from me.

Leenck didn't answer, nor did he stop walking.

"I know you are sick," I said.

Leenck stopped and turned around. "What?"

"Dude, I know you a sick muthafucker. You drink all day long."

Leenck didn't respond. He stared at me and then turned and began walking again.

"I'm just kidding with you, man. Jesus. What's up with you? I'm just joking with you."

"I'm sick. I'm really sick."

Another of the Frisbee kids yelled "Fuck!" followed by "This Frisbee is fucked up!" followed by "Who the fuck even makes this shit-ass Frisbee!"

Leenck likely had no idea why he had admitted to me that he was sick. He just kept walking. Later I discovered he had not told anyone he was sick, and I was probably the last person on earth to whom he had imagined telling this particular fact. It took him about eight minutes to get to his house. He felt feverish. He felt warm, flushed almost. When he got to his kitchen, he fixed himself a mimosa. He felt sweaty, and the fever seemed to be consuming him then. He took off his shirt and realized it was wet with sweat. He had walked home slowly, so he hadn't expected this. He stripped down in the kitchen to his underwear. Sweat ran down his temples. As he walked into the living room, the doorbell rang. Leenck probably wasn't thinking. He opened the door to find me staring at him. Leenck stood in his own doorway half naked and covered in sweat. He swayed slightly while standing there. He must have known then that he was collapsing. It started in his knees. As I watched him pass out, it seemed to happen so slowly I began to wonder if something was, in fact, wrong with my own head. I barely caught him. I carried him to his couch.

"You okay, man?"

"What?"

"You passed out cold, man. You just fell."

"Where? Where am . . ."

"You're on your couch. I caught you before you hit the floor, man. I carried you over here."

"Get out."

"Wow, you're a really thankful guy."

"Seriously, you have to get out."

"What, you think I never seen a guy in his underwear?"

"You need to . . ."

"Man, I was joking about you being sick and all. But you really are sick. You need to see a doctor."

"I have already been to doctors."

"But you are sick and should probably see a new doctor."

"I am sick. And I'm dying."

"That's just the sickness talking smack, man."

"No, listen to me. Everything dies, and now I am dying." It sounded almost as if he were in a movie reciting a script. The poison had set in and in the next scene he would be clutching his chest while he vomited up yellow-green foam. This was melodrama at its finest, but he could not stop himself. And some part of me enjoyed it then.

I looked at Leenck and tried my best to select the right words: "I know of an old woman. You need to go see the old woman, Cassie. She can help you."

"No one can help me." Again, Leenck continued the drama with his short outbursts, declaimed as if he were on a stage. Why does a man speak like this? I couldn't stop myself then from thinking in that way.

"Cassie can," I said. "She cures all kinds of people. I can take you to her. She lives not far from where I grew up. All we have to do is fly to Antigua or St. Lucia and then charter a boat."

"I'm not going anywhere."

Days later, Leenck felt better. The sweats had passed. He got up, showered, and went outside. He pulled the plastic lounge chair from out of the shade and positioned it at the bottom of the few steps to the patio, positioned it in direct sunlight and then lay down on it. I watched him position that old tattered lounge chair. I could tell he was feeling better.

"Why you all naked in your backyard, you perv?" I called out to him from my side of the fence.

"Why are you looking through a crack in the fence into my backyard? So, really, who's the pervert here?"

I laughed when I heard this. He was good at making me laugh. Sometimes I forget that, that Leenck could make me laugh. "Man should be able to do what he wants in his own place," I said. And before Leenck could answer, I had climbed over the fence into his backyard. "You okay, man?"

"I'm fine. I didn't collapse or anything. I walked out here, and I can walk back inside," Leenck replied.

I walked over and sat down on the steps to Leenck's patio just behind him. "Good."

"Do you often sit down with your neighbor when he's buck-ass naked in his backyard?"

"You're the one who's naked!" I told him.

"But it is my backyard, my own place. Remember? Man should be able to do what he wants in his own place." When he said this, he mimicked my voice and the pattern of my speech but, for some reason I cannot explain even now, I did not seem to mind.

"I don't have a problem with you being naked. If you want I can turn away or get something to cover you."

"Doesn't matter. Nothing exciting here. Just an average guy."

"Yeah, you not a porn star or anything." We both started laughing. "Have you thought about what I said?"

"About what, my not being a porn star?"

"Cassie, the old woman. Will you let me take you to see Old Cassie?"

"Why would I do that?"

"Because she can cure you. She has been curing people of all kinds of disease for as long as I can remember. Scary old woman, but she is a gifted healer."

"She can't help me with what I have."

"She has cured people of heart disease, diabetes, MS, even Alzheimer's. She even cures people of cancer." I watched to see if there would be a change on Leenck's face. There was none.

"She can't help . . ."

"What is wrong with you, man? What do you have?"

"It isn't important. I just know she can't help me."

Leenck got up and walked up the steps past me and into the house. As he stood in his kitchen mixing a mimosa, I, too, walked inside through the glass doors.

"Ah, your vice," I said.

"Drinking naked?"

"Nah, just the drinking."

"You're gay, aren't you, Diego?"

"Yeah, why?"

"Most guys wouldn't casually talk to another guy who is naked and drinking in his kitchen."

"You gay?"

"No, Diego. Not gay."

"Then how did you know I was gay?"

"This is California, Diego . . ."

"Oh man, I'm not coming on to you or anything."

"I didn't think you were. It is just that my being naked didn't bother you. And you have helped me and worried about me. Most men don't give a shit about other men."

For the first time since we met, I felt uncomfortable and embarrassed. I could tell the blood was rushing to my face and could feel the warmth of it in my cheeks. "I think I better go."

Leenck could see me blushing, and something inside him enjoyed the discomfort he was producing in me: "Why, because I am standing here with no clothes on? Because you keep checking out my dick? I might not be a porn star, but I can see you checking out my abs and my dick."

"Man, your skinny ass self isn't all that . . . I gotta go, man."

"Why, you getting turned on? You want some of this? You hard, Diego?" As he said this, he turned around and said: "You want my ass?"

"No, I gotta go because there is something wrong with you, man. You are not right."

You would think I would have stayed away from this man. But of course I didn't. In this, I was as predictable as Leenck was. I went back. I kept going back. You could even argue that I am still going back.

*

"We need to get started with chemotherapy."

"Shouldn't we run another test? I mean, are you 100% sure?"

"Yes, we are sure. I have scheduled you for your chemo class tomorrow. We really need to get going on this."

"How long do I have?"

"I just don't have an answer for that." As usual, when she said this, the doctor turned away from Leenck and refused to look him in the face.

"What if I do nothing? What if I don't do the chemotherapy?"

"Then you'll die." The doctor said this with a matter-of-fact tone that seemed to Leenck almost graceful. There wasn't even the slightest change in the expression on her face, which remained flat and virtually blank. She stood up from her chair and walked over to a sink and washed her hands. Leenck found this strange seeing as she hadn't examined him while she had been in the room. But he knew it was likely just another way for her to avoid looking at him.

"But even if I do the chemo I will eventually die, right?"

"Well, we all eventually die. But you don't want to die like this."

"Maybe the lab test is a mistake."

"It is not a mistake. We have gone over this already."

Leenck could hear the growing frustration in his doctor's voice. He decided to simply agree with her. He would go to the chemo class. He would tell her what she wanted to hear. Leenck knew he was good at that, good at telling people what they wanted to hear. He had been doing that for his entire life.

*

From the boat, Leenck and I could see the darkness of the island in the distance, then the island itself. It had been six months since we first met at the beach in Santa Monica. Now, here we were sailing to the small island near Antigua I used to call home. There were too many shades of blue in the ocean between the boat and the island. Each seemed like a different possibility. I kept going inside the cabin to talk to the captain. I believed Leenck understood what we needed him to do. I wanted him to go see the old healer woman who could make different illnesses disappear. But Leenck was afraid. I knew he was afraid. He wasn't afraid of the woman, but afraid of what she might do to him.

As the ship pulled closer and closer to the island, I could make out the harbor and the various boats and small ships anchored there. There was the blue water and the white and blue boats. There were the houses I remembered, crammed together on one of the hillsides in a gaudy array of colors: flamingo pinks and crayon greens, odd teals and purples. As we approached the island, Leenck told me how his father cried in their house back in the old country. He remembered telling his father that he was not a carpenter and that he was not cut out to be a carpenter, that he was leaving the town and that way of life. And he remembered his father begging him not to do it, begging him to reconsider. His father told him that he would die from the inside out if he left their way of life. And now Leenck couldn't stop talking about how that was exactly what was happening. He had blood cells going crazy in his body. The cells were moving all through his body. From the inside out. He kept saying that his father had been right, that he was dying from the inside out.

Why does a man think this way at the end? Why does he see in the past the glimmers of prophecy that likely were never meant to be prophecy? It is hard to say why. But Leenck saw then in his father's last words to him the overwhelming power of prophecy. And without even appearing to think about it, he kept saying them out loud: "dying from the inside out." I wish, in retrospect, that all there was in the air was this "prophecy," but there was more; there was me. Leenck knew I had fallen in love with him, loved him, and was deeply in love with him. He knew it. And I am quite sure he also knew he didn't love me that way and could never love me that way. Sex with a man just didn't seem like his kind of thing. And loving a man? That was beyond his comprehension. He would likely have had an easier time having sex with me than loving me. I was his friend, despite the fact he wanted no friends. And even then, it was clear Leenck could not decide if he even cared for me as a friend. But Leenck had to know. He had to know he let me love him, allowed me to fall in love with him. It had to be one of the few things Leenck could admit to himself. He allowed me to fall in love with him, and it was clear he had no idea why he had allowed that to happen.

"Nickel for your thoughts," I said while looking beyond him at the island coming into focus.

"Nothing, really."

"We should be ashore within a half an hour. My sister has already arranged for Cassie to see us."

"Oh?"

"She is a really weird old woman. Man, the stories about her are legendary."

"She's still just a woman."

"Some think she is a god."

"I'm not sure I want to meet a god."

"Well, you'll see when you meet her. That huge white house alone on that hill over there to the left is where she lives."

"I'm not going to meet her."

"Leenck, what the hell you talking about?"

"I'm not going to meet her. I told you I would come with you, but I never said I would go see the old woman."

"Leenck, you're getting sicker. You've lost twenty pounds or more since I met you."

"I wanted to see the island. I wanted to make the trip. I wanted to leave the U.S."

"You can't come this far and not see her, man."

I turned away from Leenck then and walked back inside. As I entered the cabin, I saw myself in a mirror and suddenly wanted to laugh. "Who was the sick muthafucker?" I thought. "Who is the real sick one here?" As I stared at the mirror, I became more and more angry. The captain's assistant was saying something to him, but I couldn't hear exactly what was being said. Outside, the harbor was calm. There was almost no breeze skimming across it. The sky was overcast. And out the porthole window, I saw the mountain and trees that marked this place as my home, the place where I had grown up. I didn't want to do it, but I went back up on deck to Leenck.

"Please, just meet the woman. Talk to her. You don't have to do anything else . . ."

"Diego, I am already dead."

"Stop being crazy. Why do you always have to be crazy?"

"Don't you see? Don't you see it? It caught up to me. It has been with me for so long that it has finally overcome me. I've been dying for my entire adult life. I just didn't see it."

"Please, Leenck, the boat is docked. Stop the drama. Just come see the old woman."

"I won't. I will not. I cannot leave the boat."

"Don't do this, Leenck. Don't . . ."

"I have already done it."

The water was getting dark then in the harbor under the overcast sky. The clouds were gray and looked like dark dishwater. The air was unusually still. And Leenck waited for the tears in my eyes. But the tears didn't come. Leenck knew I would cry. He wanted me to cry. And why he wanted this I doubt he could even explain to himself. But he wanted me to drop to my knees and beg him to go see the old woman, tears streaming down my face. I am quite sure he thought it would come to that.

I don't remember how I had the strength to do it, but I turned from Leenck and made my way on to the dock. I did not turn back. I did not look back. I walked away at a slow and steady pace. And Leenck sat there coughing while seagulls scurried around on the dock fighting and arguing over garbage. And then the wind picked up, the wind suddenly sweeping the crushed plastic cups from the dock into the water. And instead of thunder, all I heard was the sound of palm trees, the hundreds of fronds rustling in the distance, the too-numerous-to-count palm trees tilting their fronds like flags in the wind. Leenck could see me in the distance then, the tiny outline of me. I could feel him watching my outline moving away from him, watching to see if I would turn around to look for him on the boat. I bet he wondered if I was crying. Later I would hear how at that point Leenck felt tired, that he felt odd, that his chest was heaving more than normal. I know he watched my tiny outline get smaller and smaller. And I never turned to look back at him. The only tears were the tears that surprised Leenck's own face. I am told the tears came quickly and frightened him. But I didn't care to hear any of this. I am told that not once had he cried in the previous twenty years.

The harbor got darker then. And my own eyes stung. There was not a single rumble of thunder, just the breeze rustling the palm trees and the seagulls going mad over debris. The rain came down. It was forceful, cool and prickly as it hit all of us on our heads and faces. Did Leenck move inside the cabin? No. Supposedly, he sat there in the rain instead. He didn't move. He was completely wet, the tears on his face indistinguishable then from the rest of his wet face. I want to believe his chest tightened in a way he had never experienced in his life. I want to believe that. What I know clearly is that the rain pelted everything, and the deck, the dock, the very earth between the boat and my father's small house, suddenly took on the dark stain of rainwater, a stain not quite as dark as the heart, a stain not quite as dark as blood. And the trees in the distance seemed to be blurring into the landscape, everything bleeding together. And again, I thought of turning back to look for the figure of Leenck on his knees, sobbing. There are times when I believe he kept staring into the distance looking for the shape of me, but even if he had he couldn't have seen me at such distance. Time and distance change everything. Years later, I am still trying to convince myself of that.

VII. Jewels

That Carlitos had killed his brother Pedro Blanco was never in dispute. Flora Diaz had predicted it. Javier Castillo felt a great amount of guilt about it. And I am somehow the one charged with remembering it. But what the Court could not decide was whether or not it was premeditated. It is never easy to believe a thirteen-year-old boy could plan his own brother's death, but so much of what I have told you by now must seem difficult to believe. Not even Carlitos himself could tell you with any certainty whether or not he had planned the whole thing.

What the Court knew was that one afternoon, a very ordinary afternoon, Carlitos struck his brother Pedro in the back of the neck with a branch from the stunted royal poinciana tree growing in his front yard, one with a sharp enough spike to puncture the right carotid artery. That his brother fell to the ground in the front yard with blood squirting from his neck, each beat of his heart propelling the blood across the dying grass in a thin arc, was never discussed. Not even the court knew these additional details. What they knew was that Carlitos struck his brother in the neck and killed him. The blood pulsing, the dying grass, the shak shak tree standing behind them witness to it all, Carlitos standing there holding the branch as if he were paralyzed, the sun disappearing from the sky then, twilight and shimmering, the way he kept yelling at his brother to get up, to stop this crap, to stop it, get up—the court knew none of that.

"Carlos! Get up! I am not going to call you again. You need to get up and do your walk now!" Every morning at 10:30 a.m., the doctor's assistant would come and fetch Carlitos. The walk lasted exactly thirty minutes, and the path was the same one used each and every day—always the same path, always the same route. This assistant, Bill, was a wiry Asian man who, to Carlitos, looked nothing like a Bill. He was clean, clean-shaven like a Bill, but a Bill was some white guy wearing a preppy shirt, one called Biff by his friends. Some Asian dude should not be named Bill. It wasn't that the name Bill was too white but that to Carlitos it seemed like a fraudulent name. He, Carlitos, couldn't escape his own name and the fact of how it marked him, preceded him. Carlos Drogón Blanco, son of Ricardo and Rosa, called Carlitos because he was smaller than he should have been up until about six years of age. Carlos Blanco was a name that one could not escape from the way Carlitos believed the name Bill allowed this Asian man to do. Carlitos wanted desperately to ask if Bill was a nickname, an English name. He wanted to know if fake-Bill had another name, a valid name.

"Get up, Carlos! Get up! I know you can hear me. Doctor says you have to do this, and that is what you have to do." The do at the end of the sentence went on and on: Carlitos heard it as do-oo-ooo-oo, the "o" almost endless through the plexiglass window in the middle of the inside door to his room. So Carlitos got up, went to the door, looked through the plexiglass at fake-Bill and then watched as he unlocked the door. Fake-Bill had been helping take care of Carlitos for about six months at that point. Carlitos knew it was only a matter of weeks before someone new would show up. These assistants never lasted more than seven months. Somewhere around the six-month mark, they would be promoted, or fired, or they would quit. Carlitos had lost track of how many assistants he had seen over the years. The constants were the doctor, the red-headed woman who dropped off his mail, and the dark-skinned man who appeared and disappeared outside his door, a man with grayish brown eyes for whom he had no name.

Fake-Bill was not a constant, but at least he was consistent. He would talk to Carlitos in the same way, in a dull and almost patronizing way. Carlitos liked that. Fake-Bill didn't try to understand Carlitos, didn't try to glean something via his eyes or his expression. Many of the previous assistants would try to keep notes, try to decipher the expressions on his face or the way he moved his eyes. Each wanted to find a way of understanding this man who had killed his own brother. Each wanted a prize of some kind, a prize like Carter and others received for deciphering hieroglyphics on tablets from Ancient Egypt. One by one, these assistants would give up. But fake-Bill never tried anything like that. He just showed up and did his job.

"You know the drill, Carlos. Hand, please. And yes, you have to wear the strap." Strap is what fake-Bill called the leash that attached the handcuff he placed on Carlitos' wrist to the belt around fake-Bill's waist. Even though the grounds were fenced, this was a requirement. And fake-Bill was right; Carlitos knew the drill. But that day, Carlitos did not want to put on the handcuff. And maybe, in some odd way, Carlitos hoped that this would somehow get him out of doing the walk, a walk that time after time filled him with more and more dread. Carlitos could detail for you how many azalea bushes and how many hydrangeas lined the south walk. He could tell you that at the time of his walk, at that time of year, that the oak casts a shadow across the third concrete block from the end of the long sidewalk. He could even tell you that the jays would be there the following week and would be territorial and aggressive because of the newly hatched, struggling chicks. Carlitos knew all of this, but he would never tell a soul.

After the walk, what the doctor sometimes referred to as a "constitutional," Carlitos was taken back to his room. The door was locked. Fake-Bill said something about how he wouldn't see him at lunch or at afternoon games because he had an interview or something. Carlitos was only half-listening. Fake-Bill continued rambling about an interview, and Carlitos could tell from the tone in his voice that fake-Bill was nervous about it, cared deeply about the outcome of it. But other than the tone of his voice, Carlitos didn't pay too much attention to the particular words fake-Bill used. What registered were a few words: *interview, important, school,* and the one that stood out the most, *psychiatry*. When Carlitos looked back toward the door, all he saw was fake-Bill's back as he exited the outer doors of the hallway that led to his single room with its single bed, its one chair, its one small table, and a sink above which hung an old mirror and a shelf with one coffee mug, one plastic glass, and his sad toothbrush next to one small tube of toothpaste.

The red-haired woman would arrive in an hour or so, as she always did, and place his mail in the bin by the outside door at the end of the short hallway to his room. She never so much as waved or said a word. She just opened the outside metal door, held it open with her foot, dropped the mail in the bin, and then stepped back through the door. Within seconds there would be the deeply reliable sound of the door jam as she tugged the door to make sure it was locked. If he had mail, it wouldn't be retrieved from the bin and given to him until after lunch. The caretakers and assistants knew that to let Carlitos read any of his letters before lunch might lead to a difficult meal. The letters often riled Carlitos up. They made him act out. They made him even crazier than everyone already thought he was. The one aspect of these letters no one discussed, not even the doctor, was the fact they all came from one person, his mother.

11 May

Dear Carlitos,

Old Flora Diaz is dying. The old *bruja* is finally dying. I am convinced of this. She is ashen and her face sunken. She looks as if she needs help, but I would never help or do anything for that horrible old woman. Look at what she did to you and your Father! I know that as well as I know anything. I know she will be dead soon, will be in Hell soon. She never went to Mass, that Flora. She never went once in all the years I have lived here. And she should suffer in Hell for all of the evil things she has done. Not even Guadalupe can help her now.

The doctor says you have been doing well lately. You know you need to do well, Carlitos. You need to learn to follow the instructions of the people there. It is for your own safety. You cannot be stubborn. You have to remember how lucky you are to be alive. God spared you so I wouldn't have to cry more than I already do. God spared you death despite what you did. And you need to be thankful for that.

I pray for you each and every day, *mijo*. And I pray you don't end up in Hell. All we can hope is that our Pedro speaks to God on your behalf and reminds God it was an accident, reminds Him that you didn't mean to do it, to kill him. Will you tell me that? Will you tell me, your only mother, that it was an accident? I know it was an accident, but could you tell me this? I know I ask a lot, but because of your carelessness I lost a son. Do you ever think of that? I lost one of my sons.

Okay, I will close the way I always do, by telling you I love you and by telling you I am praying for you. Be good for the people there. Please *mijo*, be good.

Rosa always ended her letters to Carlitos with "*amor y besos.*" It was the only time where her desire to use English correctly could not be implemented. Javier Castillo understood this, and I understood it. In that moment of closure, one returns to one's original language. Each time Javier Castillo recounted this story, he always emphasized this point. "*Amor y besos*" was more than a term of endearment to him. It was a kind of quiet rebellion against English. But now, the more I think about this, the more I really think on this, the more even I believe closing in Spanish is just another kind of defeat. Original language? Which of us can remember that now? The Europeans came to steal from us. They came with their Spanish and then their English and, in the process, tried to erase all of our languages, so much so we cling to Spanish, the lesser of the two evils, the one we were forced to learn first.

Rosa might not have thought about any of this the way I did or Javier did, but to close a letter with English was akin to abomination to her. And it made Carlitos crazy, despite the fact he also understood this better than almost anyone his mother knew. Everything about Rosa Blanco's letters made Carlitos angry. Several times per week these letters arrived, and each and every time they were essentially the same. She prayed. She wanted him to admit killing Pedro was an accident. She was suffering. It was as if all he needed to do was read the first paragraph. That was the only part of the letter that changed from letter to letter. One could read a letter from two years ago or the one that would arrive two days later—they would both be essentially the same. And yet, despite this, Carlitos always read the entire thing. No one else wrote to him. He had no one else. The letter was as much a part of his routine as fake-Bill or the daily walk.

Carlitos did not behave himself at lunch. He often didn't. He ate, at most, four bites of his sandwich and then started throwing the rest of it across the small dining hall, at which point he was promptly returned to his room. He long ago discovered that this was a surefire way to get sent back to his room. He hated lunch. It was the only meal where he had to sit with the crazies and watch them all try to be normal. He wanted none of it. Breakfast and dinner were always brought to him in his room. And he would bet money that the reason lunch was in the dining area and not dinner had more to do with lack of staffing at dinnertime than anything else. And in this, Carlitos would be one hundred percent correct. At lunchtime, the entire staff was there. And even though Carlitos had no idea exactly how many people worked at the facility, he had somehow figured this out. Carlitos was a clever boy. He was always figuring things out.

Lunch was the bane of his existence. He had been sitting across from the guy who had raped his sister and then cut out her tongue so she couldn't tell anyone about it. Carlitos couldn't understand how anyone could be so stupid as to cut out someone's tongue with the notion that this could stop them from "talking." Things like this never worked, not even in the movies or old books. Tongue or no tongue, the truth always came out. Didn't we know this? Don't we know it still? When the rapist realized this very fact an hour after cutting out his sister's tongue, he tied her up and killed her, stabbed her twenty-two times. The lawyers had argued insanity and the Court spared him death for a life in prison. But he couldn't be placed in prison. Like it had with Carlitos, the Court deemed the rapist mentally unfit to be in prison. The rapist had heard voices, had been instructed to cut his sister's tongue out, had been instructed to thrust the large butcher knife he found in the kitchen into her chest over and over. One of the guards told another guard that the rapist went so far as to eat the tongue he cut from his sister's mouth.

Most of the other patients at the facility didn't know the whole story about how the incestuous rapist ended up with them, but very little escaped Carlitos. Many assumed he was dumb, and they said unbelievable things within earshot of him, things they would never say in front of other patients. But the rapist was making terrible smacking noises as he ate, which he often did, chewing with his mouth open in a slow and methodical way so that the food could be seen going from solid to less solid states, his large tongue slowly moving the chewed-up food around in his mouth. And Carlitos was convinced the rapist was doing it on purpose to annoy him. Some ham smeared with mustard, pulled from the uneaten portion of his sandwich and thrown across the table, put a quick and clean end to the situation. Carlitos was back in his room within six minutes.

With the exception of the walk and the lunch, Carlitos spent the majority of his day locked in his room. He had no telephone or television. All he had was an iPad, the gift of a philanthropic organization. The doctor had to approve any downloads of apps for it. No streaming video and, since the Internet connection in the patient areas was limited and controlled, no email either, not that Carlitos had anyone to email. To even download an app, Carlitos had to make an appointment with the doctor's secretary. What Carlitos was supposed to use the iPad for was to read books. Mostly, he played a game with exploding jewels. At night, he would use an app that showed the night sky and the stars. He would lie on his back in the dark of his room with his iPad raised over his face at arm's length looking at the constellations. As with the jays and the shadows, he had grown aware of when to expect certain constellations. He knew all of the constellations: Scorpio, Orion the hunter, the Pleiades clustered and buried within Taurus. He had that kind of a mind.

Carlitos preferred keeping a journal on his iPad, despite the fact they provided him pencils and notepads. The notepads were never a problem, but the pencils were always tricky. Sometimes, the pencils seemed to elongate before his very eyes into spears and stakes. They would transform into branches in his hand, branches with spikes and thorns and all manner of jagged and pointed things. Transformations: they seemed ever present in Carlitos' life. The pencils, the way his reflection sometimes morphed so that his face, at times, looked more like his dead brother's face, the way the air just outside his plexiglass door sometimes shimmered and then darkened and darkened until it was a man watching him, staring at him. What Carlitos could not understand was why these transformations never happened with, say, his toothbrush. The toothbrush always remained a toothbrush. But pencils, well they sat in the corner of the room in their box. He couldn't use them. He wouldn't look at them. He would have preferred they took them away altogether.

Once every few weeks, Carlitos would be summoned to see the doctor. It had been the same doctor for the entire time he had been there. The doctor would ask him questions and then watch for a change of expression. It was almost always the same. "Have you had any dreams, Carlos? Any visions of odd things? Are you keeping your journal?" Carlitos' face remained unchanged. He would never describe the things he had seen, the transformations, the man who every so often seemed to materialize out of thin air to stare at him through the plexiglass for sometimes as long as twenty minutes before fading away, the man with the grayish-brown eyes who always had what Carlitos felt was the deepest concern etched on his face, the man who never so much as spoke a word to him. Who was this man? Carlitos felt quite certain he had seen the vanishing man when he still lived at home. He felt he had seen him outside Church sometimes when he and his mother and brother were leaving mass. He felt he had seen him just beyond the dusty schoolyard that seemed incapable of growing grass. But Carlitos distrusted his memory. And who could blame him?

Sometimes, the doctor would ask if he had gotten any interesting news from his mother. Other times he asked whether or not Carlitos wanted to see a priest. For this, and this alone, Carlitos would offer a response. He would slowly rotate his head left to right and back to the left. "No? You still don't want to see a priest? Your mother always asks if we can let you see a priest . . ." Again, Carlitos twisted his head. And again, the doctor would sigh and jot a few words on the paper in Carlitos' chart. As he wrote, Carlitos stared at the doctor's pen. He didn't do this to see if it would transform into a branch or switch but to decipher what the doctor scribbled in the chart, the chart that had grown larger and larger with time, the one labeled CARLOS DROGÓN BLANCO, No. 0167 in yellow and white plastic tape. That day, the doctor wrote: "Status unchanged. Responds with head nod No. No other response. Remains mute."

When Carlitos lined up three jewels of the same kind on his iPad, they would explode and new jewels would fall into the excavated space. If he lined them up like an L, they exploded in a different way. As they exploded, Carlitos felt he could almost make out markings in the background of the screen, small etchings or hieroglyphs. But he could never remember them long enough to string them together, to construct the message he was certain was there behind the jewels. The jewels exploded and the small traces of light then faded away. And then there were new jewels. Father Happy had told Carlitos that every living soul was like a jewel in God's eyes. And somewhere buried deep within Carlitos, this resonated each and every time the jewels exploded, though he couldn't explain this to anyone, much less himself. Beautiful jewel, Father Happy called Carlitos. Beautiful jewel. Carlitos had been ten when he first pulled his t-shirt over his head and pushed his hands into his underwear attempting to get the priest's attention. He had no words then to explain to himself why he needed the priest's attention. But there on the screen of the iPad, the only beauty was when row upon row of jewels exploded like fireworks and then twinkled like stars. No priest. Carlitos absolutely did not want to see a priest, any priest.

One night, as Carlitos was trying to fall asleep, as he played round after round of Jewels, he saw the shimmer outside his inside door. It was subtle, not quite a flash of light but definitely light almost flickering. There, as so many times before, was the man with the brown skin. Carlitos sat up assuming the man would disappear once he took a different position on the bed. But he was still there standing in the short hallway leading from the outer door to the inner door of his room. He turned on the light and found, to his surprise, that the man was still there staring at him. Carlitos got up from his bed and walked toward the door with the expectation the man would vanish. But he didn't. Carlitos studied the man, and the man studied Carlitos. The straight nose, the dark skin, the light brown eyes flecked with gray: we know full well this was no apparition. And try as he did, Carlitos could not place where he had seen this man before. Why did he keep dreaming this man into existence outside his inner door, always outside his door and never inside the actual room? The two men stood there staring at each other until Carlitos tired of it and returned to his bed. He continued watching the dark man until, as he always did, he faded away leaving only the short hallway to the outer door in his place.

Fake-Bill arrived on schedule after a few days' absence. "Carlos! Get up! You know what time it is." Carlitos walked to the door and received the acrylic handcuff and the strap. He walked with fake-Bill down the path, around the stone garden and then down the main walk and back. The birds were fairly silent, something that seemed strange. It was as if half or more of the birds had disappeared. And there were no jays around to have bullied the other birds, to scare them off. Carlitos looked all around for the jays. The jays were supposed to be there, practically everywhere, by then. The lone long branch that hung over the walkway, the one that littered the walk in the fall and shadowed it at this time of year, the one that almost without fail would be perch for a bird or two at this hour, was empty. This did not seem right. He followed the branch from the central trunk of the tree out, out, tracing each branch branching into smaller branches, but there wasn't a single bird in the tree. There was always a bird there at this time of year; Carlitos knew that. He knew that it was not necessarily the same bird, but there was always a bird there. As they approached the door to the wing where Carlitos stayed, fake-Bill announced: "It's my last day, Carlos. They have been training my replacement, and the doctor will introduce you to him tomorrow, Monday at the latest. I got into med school. Not that you care or anything, but just wanted to tell you."

Carlitos stopped and stared at fake-Bill and, for the first time, fake-Bill saw a living man inside Carlitos' eyes. What fake-Bill expected was anger or rage, but what he saw was something closer to fear or panic. Fake-Bill knew in that moment he would be a great psychiatrist. He knew it as surely as anything. He had cracked the mute who refused to show his cards, the poker player who never gave a thing away with his expression.

Fake-Bill was sure of it, sure he had seen panic in Carlitos' face, his eyes. Yes, he knew he was destined for greatness after all. "So, come on Carlos. Let's get you back to your room."

The following day, after the guy who normally worked weekends showed up and took Carlitos on his walk, after the interminable lunch that he should have ended with a quick throw of food but didn't, after the letter from his mother and news of a distant relative being sick, he was summoned to the doctor's office. "Carlos, this is Raúl Sanchez, one of my new assistants. We have assigned him to you, and he will be helping to take care of you from now on. As you know, William has left us for better things."

"Carlos, I go by Pedro, so you can call me Pedro."

"Mr. Sanchez . . . He is the one, remember? He won't call you anything. He will never utter a word to you."

"I know, sir. But I just wanted him to know."

"All he ever does is turn his head to say no. And he only does that when you ask him to see a priest. Otherwise, you get nothing from this one."

"I understand, sir. I just . . . Well, I just wanted to say what I would say to any of the other patients."

"You will soon see that this kind of thing is a waste of time."

"Yes, sir. I am here to learn and improve my skills."

Carlitos was escorted back to his room by Raúl-who-was-to-be-called-Pedro. Pedro spoke to him the entire way, something fake-Bill and the others never did. At times, Pedro spoke to him in Spanish to see if that elicited more of a response than English did. But Carlitos didn't respond. "You know, Carlos, I am here for you. However you want to talk, we can talk. I know you write, so if you want you can write me a letter. Anything you want to do, we can do." Pedro watched for a response from Carlitos, but there was no response. Once he had deposited Carlitos in his room and locked the door, Pedro started to walk off but turned around and came back to the door. Unlike most assistants who just yelled loudly enough to be heard through the door, through the plexiglass window, Pedro picked up the two-way telephone.

Carlitos stared at him in disbelief but walked over and picked up the phone on his end. "Forgot to say I'll see you tomorrow for your walk. You know, this phone thing is kind of cool. It's like a walkie-talkie or something. It reminds me of when I was a kid. I used to connect cans together with a string . . ." Carlitos dropped the phone and backed away from the door without ever taking his eyes off of Pedro. He kept asking him to pick up, but Carlitos refused. The new assistant eventually tired of trying and then hung up his end and walked away. The phone inside Carlitos' room dangled like a small weight on a string. Carlitos wouldn't hang it up; he wouldn't even go near it. He stared at it and furrowed his brow. He backed away from it, from the door, until he could feel the side of the bed behind his knees. He sat then and continued to stare at the phone, the receiver in that moment looking like a musical note suspended in air.

That night, as Carlitos lay in bed holding the iPad up toward the ceiling with both hands, he tried to find Scorpio, which he was convinced he should be able to see at that time of year. He tilted the iPad in every direction looking for it, but it was nowhere to be found. How could this man, named Pedro of all things, show up today? Why was he here? Pedro, his brother's name. Why now? Why had his brother chosen now to come back? Carlitos could not, for the life of him, find Scorpio. It should be there in its usual location, it should be there at this time of year. He followed the stars, each of the small lines of branching stars that should lead toward Scorpio, and found nothing remotely resembling Scorpio. Someone had stolen it, murdered it. He shifted the iPad above his head in direction after direction for almost an hour before giving up. After what seemed like hours in the dark lying perfectly still, he knew he wasn't going to fall asleep, and he began playing the jewel game. His dead brother had taken the form of this new assistant, an assistant who wanted to be called by his dead brother's name. His dead brother had taken human form and wanted to talk on the phone. Surely this was a terrible sign.

Up until that day, the only way Carlitos had ever seen Pedro was outside in the garden. Pedro chirping the same short staccato notes in sequence; Pedro hopping sideways on a branch tapping-out a kind of Morse code: these were the things to which he had become accustomed. And there in front of him, as a column of jewels exploded and caused an adjacent row to explode as well, Carlitos saw the letter P form and then disappear. He didn't speak then. He didn't even try. But he cried. The sounds that escaped his mouth weren't perfect English or even a poor Spanish. They were guttural and dark, as if they were part of a language so old it didn't yet have syllables. The vocal cords, which up until then had been dried, desiccated, sick with immobility, suddenly worked. Carlitos cried and grunted a string of muted, dull coughs and chokes. And these sounds scared Carlitos, who hadn't heard his own voice since that afternoon so long ago when he had screamed "Get up! Get up!" He cried, and row after row of jewels kept exploding on his screen, each explosion blurred and streaked by his wet eyes. But he kept playing. Why now? Carlitos choked and sobbed. He shook with fear. And on the screen of his iPad, the jewels continued falling into place, exploding in a panic and falling like stars, like those rare stars you sight on a summer night, the ones you only see when you are alone.

VIII. The News

The potted ficus in the corner of Flora Diaz's kitchen, barely four feet tall and planted in a rust-colored ceramic pot, the one she watered every six days had, for the first time in almost four decades, started showing some yellowing leaves. This had not escaped Flora Diaz's attention, nor had it escaped Javier Castillo's attention. He made a point of describing these leaves when he first told me about that particular time in his life. The leaves were yellowing, not browning and falling off to be replaced by new leaves. This ficus had grown large, was one of the only things Flora Diaz brought with her to California when she left the island. She knew that *Ficus benjamina*, the weeping fig, only offered up yellowing leaves in times of stress, of over-watering or under-watering. And Flora Diaz was quite certain she had not altered the routine she had adopted in caring for this plant. As she studied the ficus, she discovered a whitish patch, discovered that one of the three thinner trunks twisting together to make the substantial trunk had a white ring roughly midway between the soil of the pot and its umbrella of branches. She noted this but could not discern the significance of it, and this bothered her more than she realized.

Sitting at her kitchen table after performing her morning ritual of checking her plants and drinking a glass of hot water with a freshly crushed pepper in it, Flora Diaz could feel a prickling on her skin followed by a subtle change in the light just in front of her. Then came the distinct smell one associates with a burning wire. The light elsewhere in the kitchen was merely the warm light entering through the windows, but the cool-white light she could appreciate in front of her was not natural light. It was anything but natural. It was her nephew Javier Castillo. As she spoke his name, his form began to take shape, the cool-white light suddenly variegated and shimmering and then the shape of his head and his arms shaded, shaded and then definitely there. Within another thirty seconds or so, Javier Castillo was sitting in the chair across from his aunt, and ten or so seconds later he was solid enough to speak.

"I can never surprise you, Tía. Can I? Like Mama, you can sense me before I am completely here."

"Why are you here, Javi?"

"Is that any way to greet your only nephew?"

"No games today, Javi. I am not in any mood."

Flora Diaz was not one to waste time with small talk, I was told, even with members of her own family. The time for small talk was gone, was something she left behind when she left the island. She was not interested in pleasantries. She wanted the bare minimum, the facts. Her nephew was a reminder of her past, no matter how much she tried not to think of him in that way. She knew he had nothing to do with her early difficulties, but she couldn't help but feel this way. In this, her family was no different than others. Javier Castillo was a reminder of her sister, of the life they had as children, of the island she grew up on, the fact she came from a long line of "difficult people." He reminded her of her own mother, his nose most definitely hers. And, sadly, he reminded her of the Archbishop who had time and time again abused and violated both her and her sister so many years prior. The smile, that mouth, the way it was capable of deception: Javier Castillo had his father's mouth which, to Flora Diaz, negated the regal nose he had inherited from her side of the family.

"I'm here because, because Mama is dying," Javier said.

"No. She is not. I would know such a thing."

"Well, she is dying. She's lost almost thirty pounds over the past two months alone."

"Nonsense," Flora said. I am sure she believed this was a trick, an elaborate trick. Considering her nephew and his significant skills in manipulating people, she had to have considered this.

"I think she has something . . . cancer, something."

"Not possible." Flora Diaz waved her hand as if swatting gnats, but there was nothing in the air except the occasional and awkward silence after each of them spoke.

"Mama won't even see people, Tía. She won't heal anyone."

"Because she is a selfish whore trying desperately to heal herself."

"See. This confirms you know she is sick."

"I don't know anything. What I do know is that you are reckless. You are never satisfied. You manipulate. You are far too clever for your own good."

Flora Diaz was probably not surprised at these thoughts she had, but she had to be surprised she was voicing them to her nephew. She was mostly a private person who said little, but she couldn't stop herself then.

"I have, at many times, been a mother to you. And how did you repay me? You persuaded the Blanco man down the road to follow you. And for what? Because you need to be adored, to be worshipped? You let him see you disappear. You charmed him despite the fact you knew it would lead nowhere. You . . ."

"Tía, it is just plain rude to look into other people's lives like that!"

"You are a charmer, Javi. You have done this before and will continue to do it. You choose to charm . . . You choose to do this."

"Tía, we are all capable of charming, as you call it. It is the one thing that we can all do. Why can't you admit this has nothing to do with my charming someone? What upsets you is the fact I charmed a man."

"Don't start that with me, Javi. I know what you are, and I have never so much as said a word to you about it."

"But it bothers you. I know it does. It bothers both you and Mama. My behavior reminds you of someone neither of you will ever discuss. I have worked this out. I remind both of you of another man, one neither of you can bear to talk about."

"Go home to your mother, Javi. At least there you won't cause as much trouble as you have done here."

"The Blanco man was a mistake, I admit that. But it was years ago, Tía."

"Just forget it. It is done. No need to keep discussing it. I think it best you leave now, Javi. Go care for your mother."

I wish I had been there to watch Flora Diaz chastise Javier Castillo, but once she had gotten the outburst out of her system she went on to surprise herself further with nothing but silences. Javier Castillo was definitely not polite. As if convincing people to turn over their money to him was polite. As if using your ability to manipulate people in all manner of ways was polite. Javier Castillo was his mother's child through and through. That a man could possess the gift he had was something Flora didn't know was possible until Javier Castillo was born. That he could bend light, as her mother Tita Diaz had called it, still amazed her, though she would never admit that. Her mother couldn't do that. Not even her sister could do that. She had been taught that no woman since the first of their kind had held that particular gift. Both she and her sister had been warned by their mother not to have sons, but her sister had not listened. She was selfish and did whatever she wanted to do. And this was the result, the first man to possess one of the gifts, the most dangerous of the gifts. When Javier recounted this, he always had a sheepish and almost guilty look on his face. He knew quite certainly that he had been a mistake. And mistakes always have consequences.

Minutes passed then with not a word between the two of them. The birds outside had stopped their morning racket, the relaying of the news as Flora's mother Tita Diaz used to call it, which only made the silence in the kitchen more palpable. And Flora became very much aware then of her nephew Javier Castillo and the sadness in his face. He had come for her help, but this was one time she refused to help, could not help even if she wanted to do so.

"Mama needs you. You should have known I was coming. You should have seen me coming."

"I am not in love with my skills the way you and your mother are. She has made herself known as a healer. She should heal herself."

"That is cold, Tía, even for you."

"Not cold, Javi. Not cold at all. Just the truth."

But Flora Diaz had lied, at least somewhat. She did know Javier Castillo was coming. She had seen it weeks earlier. But what likely upset her was the fact she didn't foresee the reason why he was coming. She must have known it was because he was in trouble. But to hear Javier tell the story this was, for the first time in over three decades, a moment his aunt had not seen correctly. And this must have confused her, disturbed her. It certainly disturbed him.

"Are you okay, Tía? You seem a bit out of sorts."

"Why? Don't tell me you suddenly have the gift of Reading?"

"I don't need your gift to see the changes in your face."

"You always were a clever boy, Javi. So clever. But you are not *that* clever."

"Mama's dying, Tía. You know it as well as I do. There has to be someone in the family who can heal her. I know it isn't you, but you would know the right person."

"There is no one. We three are all that is left. There have always been at least three, three gifted fools sharing none of the same gifts. Your *abuela* could have saved her. Your *abuela* could have saved anyone. But this is irrelevant because your mother would not have the strengths she does were my mama alive."

Flora could remember as a child watching her mother tend to the sick from all over the island. And she remembered the way her sister Cassie would study her, memorizing everything she did. The way her mother cracked the window; the way she steadied her hands or shook her head; the way in which she lowered her voice: Cassie studied it all. Did she steal this skill from their mother? Or was it that Cassie already had the skill and was simply taking advantage of being able to observe a good teacher? Flora would never know, Javier would never know, though in the secret space of this story we all believe Cassie stole that gift from her mother. She was that ruthless. She was born ruthless. Flora Diaz had no gift for healing. All she had was sight, what her mother had called the gift of Reading. And that had not become fully her own until her mother had died in the time after she had escaped the convent. None of them fully appreciated their "gifts," fully commanded them until her mother died. Javier was quite sure of this. He would say that the day his *abuela* died his entire body changed, his mind changed, everything changed. It was as if the air itself surrounding him had thinned.

"Go back to your mother. She will not be happy you came here."

"Tía, you must come back with me. There must be a cousin, someone who can help her."

"I won't. I will not. I have no intention of returning to that place. Why would I fly halfway across the world and then take a boat to that horrible place?"

"There has to be another like us in the family. There must be a distant cousin, someone in the country."

"There are seven gifts, Javi, but there are only three of us left. Even if a distant cousin had skills, it would not be strong enough to help. And it would not be the gift of Healing." As she said this, Flora Diaz sighed as if worn out, as if annoyed at the ignorance of her nephew, as if by doing so he would tire and leave. "There are only three of us, Javi. We are all that is left of our kind. At one point, there were many of us, but we are all that is left now."

Javier Castillo sat still and stared at his aunt. He said nothing more. His face became determined, and he slowly faded into a shadow, and then a shimmer, and then air. It was gradual. There was the man, and then the man seen through but still there, and then the spotlessly clean wall of the kitchen behind the chair where Javier Castillo had been sitting. Flora had seen this many times. The Blanco man had seen it. I have seen it. She knew that within minutes he would be near his mother's side or God knows where else in the world. She remembered her nephew as a child, before her mother had passed. He was born in that convent. She remembered how Javier, not even five years old, demonstrated his gift, materializing to each of them in their rooms in the evenings, moving from room to room and across town without walking. And she remembered how each time he left her she could follow the thread he left in the air to see where he went after disappearing. But when she concentrated, she could not see him. She couldn't see Javier Castillo at all. Not one to give up easily, she got up, crossed the room, tore some dead leaves off the ficus and crumbled them on the table. She held her hands over them for almost fifteen minutes but saw nothing of Javier Castillo's whereabouts. No matter how she concentrated, she could see nothing of her nephew.

She had not foreseen the reason why her nephew had come to visit her, and then she could not see him at all. She kept trying. From what I have told you, you know she had to have kept trying. She must have stared so hard at the leaves crumbled on the table that she could feel the muscles on her scalp and the slim muscles along her temples begin to twitch and ache from her staring. Her mother had been the only person on earth she could not see from a distance. You know Flora had to be confused. She must have considered the possibility that Javier was as strong as her own mother. But trust me when I say this: that was just not possible. In all of this, the one thing I have learned is that none of them—Cassie, Flora, or Javier—were as strong as the old woman Tita Diaz had been in her prime.

So many links. Too many links. The first time Javier Castillo had visited Flora Diaz there in the Valley, she should have known, should have seen what was to happen. It is likely she saw the events about to unfold but wanted no part of it. He had asked about the man down the street many times. He wanted to know what he did for work. Flora was so stupid not to intervene then. But she ignored what was right there before her eyes, ignored her nephew's comments about how the man had really green eyes, the kind that startle you. He wanted the Blanco man. This I know. He wanted him. Her nephew was worse than the idiot girls she despised, the ones who threw themselves at men, tried to seduce them with coyness and guile. Yes, her nephew was, in many ways, worse than any of these girls. He wanted the Blanco man, and he was going to have him. But if you pull a link from a chain, the chain will no longer be complete. She knew this. She and her sister had pulled many links from many chains in their youth, destroyed them even.

A few days after Javier Castillo's visit, Flora Diaz was surprised by the sound of her own doorbell. When she opened the door, Carmen Jiménez was standing there with that stupid look on her face. "I am sure you knew I was coming, so I won't keep you too long." Flora Diaz ushered her to the kitchen where, as she had done countless times, she crumbled the dried leaves Carmen Jiménez brought her onto the kitchen table. With her hands over them, Flora saw nothing. Carmen was chattering on about how she might be up for a promotion but that she wanted to make sure.

But the way Javier recounts all of this, Flora Diaz saw nothing of Carmen's future, and the only aspect of Carmen's past she could see was what she had already seen years before, not sight really but plain old memory.

"So, do you see the promotion? I know you can see that I had an affair with the manager, but what's a girl to do, right?"

"I'm very tired today, Carmen. I didn't sleep well last night, and now I am having trouble concentrating."

"It's okay, girl. We all have bad days."

"Yes, come back in a few weeks."

"Well, if I haven't heard about the promotion by then, no need to come back!"

Carmen was up and out of the house in what must have seemed a blur to Flora Diaz. First the visit from her nephew; and then her inability to find him in her sight; and then the unexpected visit from Carmen Jiménez: how was this possible? Unexpected? Nothing was ever unexpected for Flora Diaz. She was the soothsayer, the fortune teller, the oracle. Though she would never have used any of these words to describe herself, they were the words others had used to label her for her entire life. Try as she must have, she had no explanation for her sudden lack of vision. Something was wrong. She could feel it in her chest. Something was terribly wrong.

Flora tried to go about her business. She swept off her front porch and noticed the histrionic Blanco woman down the block pretending not to see her. Of all people her nephew could have chosen to charm, he had to choose that crazy woman's husband. And why? Vanity, she must have thought, nothing but vanity. Javier Castillo was always such a vain boy. She went back inside. She rearranged the plants in her living room and kitchen. She went out into her backyard and weeded the flowerbeds. As she pulled the weeds, she realized that she was merely pulling them from the dirt, that she couldn't feel them the way she had her entire life. As a child, she remembered the first time she touched a plant and felt the spark in her fingertips, the way her mother had smiled at her and said, "It is okay. This is how some of us are." But there in the backyard, she felt no spark. The weeds were just weeds. They rose from the dirt with the slightest of tugs, and there was nothing more than that. The weeds rose from the ground at her insistence and clumps of dirt fell from their tangle of roots when she shook them. Something was wrong.

Flora stood up and walked around her backyard. In almost every flowerbed, weeds thrived. Several of the plants had died because the weeds had stolen too much of the water around their roots. She did not believe she had neglected her yard, but there was the evidence staring her in the face. But the evidence seemed rigged, flawed because she knew she had weeded the beds just a few days earlier. But there in front of her was an overabundance of weeds choking off her plants and flowers. She walked over to the old tree in the yard with a kind of confidence one sees in a magician who not only knows the magic trick but how to convince the audience it is every bit as real as the walls around the theater. Surely her skill was just weakened. Surely she was just out of sorts, too tired. Surely something as large as a tree . . . She touched the tree and felt only the grooved and cracked surface of the bark. Nothing more. No spark. No sudden rush of images. All of her life a tree was like an antenna for her. It amplified her ability to see with its roots extending down and out, its branches spreading out above her. But there in the yard that day, nothing. Flora Diaz backed away from the tree and, for the first time in weeks, knew in the quiet of her mind that something was, in fact, terribly wrong.

Flora heard bells. She became aware it was someone ringing her doorbell over and over repeatedly. Carmen Jiménez must have left something and had come back to retrieve it. But again, she hadn't seen Carmen coming. When she answered the door, she was faced not with Carmen Jiménez but with Rosa Blanco, the woman who lived down the street. Flora did not invite her in.

"You may have fooled everyone that lives around here, but you haven't fooled me!"

"I would never try to fool you, Rosa."

"I know you are a wicked old *bruja*. You made my husband disappear. You did it. And you killed my son!"

"I did nothing but tell you the truth, things you didn't want to hear." Flora tried to close the door, but Rosa pushed her foot against it to keep it from closing.

"You know, it is terrible to pray for bad things, but I pray every night that you suffer the way I have."

"Everyone suffers, Rosa. Everyone. Not just you." With that, Flora had the strength to slam the door shut.

Rosa Blanco kicked the door, hit it with her fists, and continued to do so for almost three minutes. Flora Diaz sat in a chair in the corner of her living room and stared at the door. She stared at it as if by doing so she could make Rosa Blanco disappear. She tried to charm the woman from down the street to leave, but she couldn't calm her mind enough to effect the charm. But Rosa tired of hitting and kicking the door. And she eventually tired of yelling obscenities and curses in both English and Spanish. But long after the ruckus of Rosa Blanco ceased, Flora Diaz continued staring at the door. It may have been thirty minutes later, possibly even an hour, when the mail slot swung upward and the even rectangle of light in the door spit an envelope on the floor in front it. She could hear the postman walking off the porch and down the steps.

I like to believe this was a relief for her to hear the postman's predictable steps. At least those steps told her this wasn't a note from the crazy woman down the street who, as far as Flora was concerned, should be locked away in an institution like her one remaining son. Javier Castillo had charmed her husband, and the story of their lives had been changed. She knew that. I knew that. Javier changed everything around him so easily. We know that the Blanco man leaving made his wife Rosa crazy. One thing after another, the dominoes had fallen and, as they did, other dominoes had to fall. Mail usually came around 1:00 p.m. Flora Diaz left the envelope lying on the floor. How she was able to do that, to leave it there, is the one part of the story I will never completely understand. I could never have left a letter lying there like that.

Flora Diaz stood in her kitchen staring at the ficus in the corner. She could see that one of the three trunks had not just a white patch but also a full ring of white. She studied it and realized there were flecks of yellow as well. Rot. The plant had acquired rot. As she studied the other parts of the trunk, she found another ring, this time on one of the other three components of the trunk. Flora Diaz had gotten the ficus as a gift as a young girl. It was a gift from her great aunt, her mother's aunt, Clara Diaz. It reminded Flora of the plant her great aunt had kept in her own kitchen, a small tree with a twisted trunk, a ficus, the weeping fig. In Flora's mind, the ficus was her great aunt or, to be more precise, a symbol of her great aunt. And to see the ficus now with rot after so many years of care had to make Flora angry.

The way Javier explained it, Flora Diaz almost never dreamed. When she discovered that other people dreamed all the time, Flora had gone to her mother for answers. Her mother had no answers but told her not to worry about this because she had the ability to "dream" in the daytime, to dream while awake. Her mother knew little about the gift of Reading, but she knew it existed and was an important gift in her family. Flora Diaz's mother was the child of a Mover, and her mother's aunt, the one who gave her the ficus, was a Reader. But her mother and her great aunt never talked about their gifts with each other. They rarely talked at all. What Flora knew about her grandmother was the fact she viewed the English and Spanish, the white men who had claimed much of the Caribbean in times past, as devils. And though Flora never met her grandmother, she heard her grandmother's words from her mother's mouth all the time as a child. Her great aunt spoke of the devils as well.

But the night after the visits from Carmen Jiménez and Rosa Blanco, Flora Diaz supposedly had odd dreams. In one she could see trees twisting and bending and, in the branches of a very large shak shak tree, her nephew was sitting and clutching the branches as the tree swayed, its obscene elongated pods swinging back and forth due to heavy gusts of wind, the blood-red petals fluttering away from the tree almost as if in slow motion. When Flora woke, she couldn't shake the odd sensation that the dreams were both real and not real. What did the dreams mean? Why was Javier Castillo stuck in a tree? Was there a hurricane coming that would damage the island? This was the difficulty with dreams. One had to interpret them, which was a skill Flora Diaz did not possess.

When Flora rose from bed, dressed herself and went to the kitchen the next morning, she did what she had done her entire life, she boiled water and crushed a pepper in a glass with the back of a tablespoon. She poured the hot water over the crushed pepper and let it sit a minute or two. Her mother had taught her this as a young girl, taught her by example. The pepper was to clear the chest and the mind. After so many years, the powerfully hot pepper barely made her tongue tingle. I never saw Javier do this. If my memory serves me correctly, only his mother and aunt did this faithfully, though he admitted he did it almost every day as a child. As Flora Diaz drank the hot water that morning, she looked over at the ficus, her weeping fig, and saw quite clearly that the rot had spread to all three of the individual trunks twisted together to make up the trunk of the plant. As she stared at the ficus, she had to have seen that many of the leaves had yellowed specks on them. Rot. Someone had brought rot into her house. One of the many people who brought leaves for her to read had brought it into her house. And try as she might, she couldn't see who had done it.

After an hour at the kitchen table thinking and rethinking the events of the past two weeks, Flora decided she should get some of her daily errands out of the way. As she walked through her small living room, she saw the letter that had been delivered the previous day lying on the floor in front of the door. She had forgotten it had come. No other mail had come, so the lone letter seemed all the more pronounced lying there on the hardwood floor. She crossed the room and picked up the letter, tore it open unevenly. She pulled the white paper from the bluish-tinged envelope and read it standing there in front of the door.

TELEGRAM

Mama died last night. Tried to come to you to tell you but unable. Not sure why. Unable to travel. Sister Juan Martín sent this for me.—Javi

Why was Javier Castillo unable to come to her? How had Flora Diaz of all people not felt her sister's passing, which now, had taken place days prior? She had not foreseen any of this. Her mother and grandmother's hushed whispers came to her, but she had to have remembered those whispers in their negative versions: "the white men won, they had finally won." As she stood there, one thing had to be very clear to her. There would be no more of them. There would be no more of her kind. Her sister was dead. Something had changed. Her family was now at its end. The white men had won, had finally killed them off. She stammered and paced and read the note over and over. Can you see this? She had helped Cassie all those years ago, helped her to do unspeakable things. And didn't she always know Cassie having a boy was a terrible omen, a violation of sorts? A boy. There was no one now to continue the family. Javier Castillo possessed one of the gifts, something that had been reserved for women for as long as her people had existed. But that boy would never bear children. There was no place in him to pass on a gift to another. The white men had finally won, had finally exterminated them. They had done it many years ago, but she hadn't realized it until that moment. There would be no more of them.

Flora became aware of the fact she was kneeling on the floor of her kitchen. She must have tried to see Javier Castillo back on the island in the Great House. But we all know she saw nothing. The white patches of rot now stretched inches between the soil and the canopy of branches. It involved all three of the trunks twisted together. I would wager money that she touched the leaves of the ficus then and concentrated but saw only the kitchen around her. The light in the windows flickered and shimmered as the wind moved one of the tree's limbs in the backyard. She must have believed it was Javier Castillo taking shape in her kitchen, but that simply would have been wishful thinking. Flora and her sister had done terrible things to their own family, even if they were only half-brothers and half-sisters. And Cassie had a boy despite being warned not to do so. And Flora Diaz must have known it was the end. She lay herself down on the floor of her kitchen, her face sticking to the linoleum, her left hand clutching the telegram. And the shadows of the large tree outside kept shifting the light as the wind moved the limbs over and over. One wonders what Flora Diaz saw as she lay there. One wonders what any of us sees at the end.

IX. The Order of Things

There were many things Alejandro Castillo did not know. For a start, he did not know his given name or the people who were his parents. In this, he was one who embraced mystery not because he had that special talent but because he had no choice. When Father Guillermo Rojas found him on the streets of that small town in Spain, the boy who became Alejandro Castillo could not even speak Spanish. He was dirty and wearing clothes that were filthy and torn. He spoke what people then believed was gibberish. Despite this, the boy had smart eyes, intelligent eyes, and a persistence in his demeanor. Father Guillermo Rojas took in the boy and raised him as his own child. Castillo, because the boy was sitting in front of the old mayor's dilapidated house that the locals in their mean-spiritedness called "the castle," and Alejandro, because Father Rojas had been reading a dense but fascinating history of Pope Alexander VI. The boy looked like a gypsy who had been abandoned by gypsies. But Alejandro Castillo was, as Father Guillermo Rojas deduced, a clever child. He learned Spanish easily and spoke properly within a year. By the age of six, one would never have known Spanish wasn't the boy's original language.

"Pardon me. Your Grace? Did you hear me? Your nephew was here asking to see you." Alejandro Castillo turned to look at his assistant. It was clear then that he had been caught in daydream. For almost a minute, the Archbishop stared at his assistant before saying a word. Why had Javier come to see him? It had been many years since he had been seen on the island. It was rumored he was living abroad. Javier brought with him a mix of emotions for Alejandro Castillo, most of which were not remotely pleasant. Javier made it a habit of creating such responses in those who knew him.

"Your Grace? Your nephew?"

"Yes, yes. I was just reviewing the events of the past week in my head."

"I asked him to come back later."

"Today? Later today?"

"Yes, Your Grace. I thought you were lying down and didn't want to simply announce him to you."

"Did he seem upset?"

Father Juan Marquez had been the Archbishop's assistant for decades. He likely had many suspicions about the Archbishop, but he was a faithful man of God who felt serving the Archbishop was his calling, his own small way of serving Holy Mother Church. In many ways, he took care of the day-to-day activities of the Church on the island. He was the one who spoke to the other two priests on the island, instructed them on finances, reviewed their sermons, etc. His voice was essentially the voice of Alejandro Castillo, the voice of the Church in that small place.

"No, Your Grace. He seemed pleasant, if not somewhat sad."

"Did he say anything?"

"No, Your Grace. Just that he needed to speak with you. Today, if possible."

"Very well."

Some men join the military to escape a life of poverty. Others join the work force, enter a life of sales and meetings like I did. But Alejandro Castillo at an early age, living with Father Rojas, saw that the Church was a kingdom on earth as much as it was the gateway to heaven. And like his namesake, the Borgia Pope, he decided early that the Church would be his escape from a common life. He entered the seminary as a teenager. And he became a priest in his early twenties, a bishop by age thirty. Others would have scoffed at accepting the role of Bishop when it was presented as something tied to moving to this island, but Alejandro Castillo had already deduced that being a bishop in a remote area would allow him to be a prince of sorts. And in this, he was one hundred percent correct. With minimal effort on his part, Alejandro Castillo convinced his elders that he should be made an archbishop instead of a simple bishop, and this gave him authority over priests on other nearby islands as well. A prince, he had transformed himself into a prince.

"I will take my lunch on the back terrace today. When Javier returns, you can bring him to me."

"Of course, Your Grace. Will he be joining you for lunch?"

"No. Send a boy to the Reynolds Estate to tell him to come at 1:30. I assume he is staying at the Great House with his mother."

"Yes, Your Grace. I have word he is at the Reynolds Estate. I will send a boy."

"Set no place for him at my table. I don't expect him to be here for very long."

"Of course, Your Grace."

Father Juan Marquez left the room as quietly as he had entered minutes earlier. And in the Archbishop's mind, the question turned and turned: why was Javier coming to see him? The boy was clever, that he knew. In this he was much like his father. Even in that instance, the Archbishop couldn't help but compliment himself. He knew quite well that Javier Castillo was not his nephew but his own son. And maybe the fact he never knew his own given name was why he allowed Cassandra Diaz to name their child Castillo. Pride, maybe, but also a strange challenge to the order of things.

The Diaz sisters were by no means the first women with whom Alejandro Castillo had sexual relations. I sometimes wonder if he slept with my own mother when she was a young woman, but my sister and I look too much like our father for me to believe that. Before and after Alejandro Castillo's vow of celibacy, the man had many indiscretions. In this, too, he was like his namesake, the Borgia Pope. But the Diaz sisters were different. In a way, he loved them more than any other women he had taken to bed. He had gone to great lengths to have them, something he had never done before or after. He couldn't remember which of the two had first caught his eye, but he knew back then they would never acquiesce to his advances the way other women had. So, because he wanted them, desperately wanted them, he convinced the Reynolds man and his jealous wife to have them placed in the convent. Alejandro Castillo was no fool. And neither was his son.

At exactly 1:15 p.m., the table on the back terrace overlooking the gardens was set with linen, silverware and china. It was a Saturday, so wine was opened and the appropriate glasses placed. Father Juan Marquez had already instructed the gardener to pick some of the purple calla lilies from the edge of the small pond, and he found them resting on the side table that sometimes served as a bar in the evenings on the rare occasion the Archbishop had guests and wanted to take after-dinner drinks and a cigar on the terrace. He quickly found a small crystal vase and placed the lilies in it with some carbonated soda water. He artfully set the three lilies pointing away from each other so that they made a triangle. Always threes because Father Juan Marquez understood the unquestionable power of that number.

At 1:25 p.m., after ensuring that everything was in order, Father Juan Marquez left the terrace and took his place in the dark entryway of the mansion to greet Javier Castillo. At 1:27 p.m., Gran Señora Hernandez brought the covered lunch and set it for the Archbishop. At exactly 1:30 p.m., Alejandro Castillo sat at the table. And a minute later, after the steward had placed the napkin on the Archbishop's lap, after the white wine had been poured and the plate uncovered, releasing its pent-up steam, after he could hear the creak of the door confirming Javier's arrival, he started his lunch.

Father Juan Marquez ushered Javier Castillo to the terrace and waved his hand toward a chair set near the table but not at the table. Before Javier Castillo sat, he said good afternoon to the Archbishop.

"You have cut your hair, Javier."

"Yes, Your Grace. It seemed the right thing to do."

"You look more like a man now with your hair short. How long have you been here?" The Archbishop continued eating his lunch of grilled chicken and rice with a mango salsa, the knife and fork clinking against the china punctuating his questions.

"Two weeks now. Mama died four days ago."

"What did you say? Died? I have heard of no funeral arrangements this week."

"Mama didn't want a funeral, much less a burial."

"Yes, but people will find out she is dead. And they will question who owns the Reynolds Estate now."

"Yes, Father. That is why I am here. I plan to stay. I need to stay. And I am her only child, but there is no will."

"And your grandfather's brother, the Governor General, is aware of this?"

"No, Father. But I need a statement from you in case he questions, something in writing to say Mama left everything to me, that I am her heir and that the estate is now mine."

"Why would I do such a thing, Javier?"

"I have never . . . asked much of you, though we both know I have every right to ask."

"A statement from me would carry little if any legal weight, Javier."

"You are a leader in the Church, Father. If you state in writing that my mother desired her belongings be left to me, it will go unchallenged."

A younger Alejandro Castillo would have been outraged, but instead he was calm and responded: "Well, I guess it is true; you have never asked much of me."

Alejandro Castillo had never done anything for his son. Javier was always quick to point that out. His stories of his father were incredible. Part of the reason he did little for Javier stemmed from the fact Cassandra Diaz had forbidden it, threatened to contact the Governor General and even Rome, if it came to that. For two years, Alejandro Castillo believed he had the upper hand when it came to the Diaz sisters. Once they were in the convent, he had them confined, beaten and tortured. How better to be their savior? How better to bed them? He made himself into their savior. It certainly was not the first time a man had done something like that. But in the end, he came to know them for what they really were: *brujas*. He came to understand that he never forced himself on either of them, much as he loved to believe he had back then, but that they had allowed the entire thing to happen, willed it to happen, he believed. At times he had to have known they had orchestrated the entire thing. Once Cassandra had delivered Javier, there within the convent's walls, everything changed. He learned with time that the Diaz sisters were powerful women, powerful in ways he would never understand. And here sat this man who was the very proof. As he looked at Javier, he had to have seen the Diaz sisters. Javier Castillo had their nose, their aquiline nose. But it was difficult for him to look at Javier Castillo and not also see himself. And this troubled him more than anything. Like his mother and aunt, Javier Castillo was a dangerous man, something wicked and untrustworthy. Like me, the Archbishop knew far more about Javier Castillo than he likely realized.

"If I do this for you, Javier, you must do something for me. You must marry."

"Marry?"

"Yes, a woman. If need be, I can find you a suitable bride."

"Mama never married, and she ran that estate just fine."

"Your mother never did the unnatural things you have done . . ."

The irony of those words must have filled Javier with rage, but Javier's face remained stony, or at least he believed his face remained stony. To Javier, his face betrayed no emotion, much less shame, which is what his father wanted from him. His father delighted in shaming him. Javier Castillo had been shamed by his father many times over his lifetime, but this was a new kind of attempt based on facts Javier Castillo felt certain, at the time, he had hidden from his father.

"Well, if you know the things I have done, then you know a marriage for me isn't going to work."

"You are manly enough. People do not stare at you the way they do those flowery boys that work down by the docks."

"I see." Javier Castillo knew then exactly to which unnatural acts his father had been referring. Although he had rarely ever seen his father or talked to him, his father had deduced that he did not love women.

"Imagine my surprise when that friend of the Governor General, the one from Italy who spent a month here with his family, confessed to me that he had fucked a man in my guest house. You were that man." Javier had never heard his father use an obscene word much less as crassly as he had just done. It was true—he did, in fact, have sex with the Italian tourist, but this was so far in the past that even the particulars of it had long since faded away. Javier would guess he had only been seventeen at the time. What confused Javier was why his father had kept this knowledge for so long without acting on it. Why had he waited until that very moment to reveal that he knew exactly the kind of man Javier was? And then, despite the fact he knew he was about to lie to his father, he said: "I will marry. For your statement, I will get married."

"Good! Don't misunderstand me. I am not saying you cannot have sex with men. We all have our particular weaknesses. But discretion . . . Discretion is, however, an important thing. And when you do have sex with men, let it be with someone like that tourist; do not go to bed with a poor field hand. Don't let a yard man fuck you. Don't sleep with poor men on this island period. They cannot be discreet. Trust me on this."

Alejandro Castillo was finished. And with a single ring of the small silver bell next to him, the Archbishop summoned Father Juan Marquez. Javier Castillo rose and politely said goodbye to His Grace before being shepherded out by the priest who assisted his father. The Archbishop sat on his terrace and quietly finished his lunch.

*

The only memory Alejandro Castillo had of the time before he was taken in by Father Guillermo Rojas in Spain, vague and refracted by the passage of time as it was, was that of being in a dense forest, a dark forest. To Alejandro Castillo, memory made the forest a cathedral of trees, the branches high above like the winged buttresses he knew in the great Spanish cathedrals. He had no idea if he had become lost in this forest or if he had been abandoned there. But in the dark crevices of his mind, the ones he refused to examine despite many opportunities to do so, he stored the belief he had been abandoned. Whether or not this was the case was irrelevant. It fueled him, the belief in this abandonment. It allowed him to do the things he had done throughout much of his adult life.

The only item Alejandro Castillo possessed from his life before being taken in by Father Rojas was a small wooden amulet. On it, there was a carving of a small axe. And there were times, like this one, where Alejandro Castillo would fish the amulet from the small ornamental box he kept atop his chest of drawers and turn it over and over in his left hand. This amulet was the oldest thing he had, the oldest thing in his small box of memories. As he turned it over and over in his hand, it conjured no memories of his life before he became Alejandro Castillo. The amulet was triangular in shape and worked smooth by its creator, smoother and smoother by time itself. The small axe was done with painstaking detail so that you could see the leather bound around the handle and, at times, even the way leather could be made to reflect light by the repeated clutching of hands, by the way repeated usage could wear down the dark skin of the leather. The old woman who had cared for Father Rojas had given it to Alejandro Castillo after the priest had died, told him it was what the priest had found in his pocket all those years ago. No money, no papers, no clues save this small wooden amulet. And as it had done his entire adult life, the amulet gave up not a scrap of information to the Archbishop.

*

Alejandro Castillo wrote the statement for his son detailing how Cassandra Diaz had left the estate to him. In what must have seemed preposterous to Father Juan Marquez, the Archbishop had requested he be taken to the Reynolds House to drop something off for his nephew. But Father Juan Marquez's job was not to question, and he arranged for the driver to take His Grace to the Great House at the bottom of Mutton Hill. When the car arrived at the house, after climbing the winding driveway from the entrance to the estate, the Archbishop asked that the driver leave him but return in half an hour.

Out behind the Great House, the cane fields and orchards stretched for miles. His son would be well off without need of the Church or anyone else. You can imagine how, at that moment, Alejandro Castillo felt a certain relief, though he would never have been able to assign such a name to that emotion he felt. Before he reached the front door, before he even crossed the entire front terrace, the door opened and a young woman lowered her head. "Señor Castillo is in the sunroom, Father." She directed the Archbishop to the sunroom, where he found his son sitting reading a newspaper. Sitting near him at the window of the sunroom looking out at the grounds drinking a cup of coffee was a young man that, from his dress, was certainly an American.

"Your Grace? I did not know you were coming."

"I wanted to drop off those papers you requested."

"Leenck, this is Archbishop Castillo, my uncle."

"A pleasure to meet you," offered the Archbishop.

The way Javier tells it, Leenck smiled and said hello. He and the Archbishop exchanged a few words, enough to confirm for Alejandro Castillo that the man was definitely from America. His English was certainly inflected with the sounds of that vast continent. It did not have the small biting consonants buried in the English spoken by the men from England, nor did it have the mellifluous rhymes inherent in Spanish or even the English spoken by those who first spoke Spanish. Alejandro Castillo told Leenck he had some family matters to discuss with his nephew and requested some time alone with him. Although presented as a request, it would have been obvious to Leenck that this was a really a command. And so, Leenck rose from his chair, slugged down the last of the coffee in his cup, and rushed from the sunroom.

"I asked you to marry and then I come here and find you with a man."

"He is not that way, Father. He came to the island to see my mother but she had already passed away. He is sick and dying and knows he won't make it back to the States."

"Oh. I just . . ."

"Assumed I was not being discreet, to use your term?"

"I have the papers. Let us focus on that."

"Well, I am glad you decided to help me. The Governor General was here yesterday, inquiring as to whether I would be staying on or not."

"Of course he inquired. His father was born in this house. He was born in this house and grew up here. It is a wonder he didn't put up more of a fight back when the rest of his family died off. But he was always deathly afraid of your mother."

"I may not have the Reynoldses' last name, but I do know my own family's history."

"I wasn't implying otherwise, Javier. I wrote up the papers. You should keep a copy of it at the bank. There are special . . ."

"Deposit boxes set up for things like that there."

"Yes. Well, I am sorry I disturbed you, Javier."

"It is fine, Father. You are the only family I have now."

"I don't think your Tía Flora would appreciate a comment like that."

"Tía Flora died, Father. She died within a few days of Mama."

The Archbishop tried to hide his surprise from Javier, and in this he was almost outstanding. But what he couldn't hide was the grief on his face. It was clear that he had loved the Diaz sisters in his own way, but his heart loved Flora Diaz more and in a very different way than it had her sister Cassie. In those confusing days in the distant past, the Archbishop had felt real heartbreak when Flora left the convent. And when she left the island it had hurt him in a way he had not anticipated. Of the two sisters, Flora was the one he likely loved, really loved. He had to have her hands bound when he visited her in the convent. And, unlike her sister Cassandra, who gave herself freely to him after the first time, he had to have Flora gagged before visiting her. Javier knew all of these things but kept this knowledge close to his chest.

"How did she die?"

"I'm not sure, but a neighbor found her in her kitchen. I suspect she had heart problems. I had seen her about a week or so before it happened."

The Archbishop excused himself, but as he was walking out, he turned to Javier Castillo and invited him to dinner the following evening. He even, as a gesture of good will, asked him to bring along the young man, Leenck. Javier Castillo had what he wanted, but he figured it best to just say yes. Alejandro Castillo was, as he had pointed out moments earlier, the only family he had left.

Dinner the following evening was to take place at 6:00 p.m. That morning, a messenger boy from the Archbishop's mansion delivered a note from Father Juan Marquez instructing Javier to be at the mansion with his guest at 5:30 p.m. for cocktails on the side terrace followed by dinner at 6:00 p.m. sharp. At exactly 5:20 p.m., the car arrived to pick them up. Shortly thereafter, from his bedroom window on the upper floor of the Archbishop's Mansion, Alejandro Castillo watched the car pass through the gates to the property and enter the grounds, watched it snake up the long driveway to the front of the house. He did not need to alert Father Juan Marquez. Father Juan Marquez was already at the door waiting to greet the Archbishop's guests. In every version of the story, Father Juan Marquez is always ready and waiting.

Javier Castillo and Leenck were seated on the shaded side terrace looking out at the sea. They exchanged small talk that betrayed they knew very little about each other. Javier didn't even know why he had taken in this foreigner who was dying. But he didn't question himself much. Death and grief inspire a different kind of loneliness, and Javier Castillo was not one to dwell too deeply on the root causes of his feelings. He rarely questioned himself at all. At 5:45 p.m., the Archbishop appeared on the side terrace and a young steward rushed out to pour him a glass of red wine. The Archbishop was not in his usual attire; he was, instead, wearing an ordinary white button-down long-sleeved shirt without the white collar and a pair of dark grey pants. He looked, for all intents and purposes, rather ordinary.

"Father Castillo . . . I mean Your Grace. I almost didn't recognize you."

"No need for formality with your uncle, Javier."

"Sir, it is good to see you again," said Leenck.

The Archbishop joined them, exchanged pleasantries and finished the glass of wine just as Father Juan Marquez showed up to call them to dinner. At exactly, 6:00 p.m., they were all seated and the first course was presented. The dinner was mostly silent save the occasional comments made by Father Juan Marquez to explain each course as it was brought to the table. After so many years, Alejandro Castillo barely heard the everyday things his assistant said. He didn't even look up at him when he spoke about things like the filet of red snapper and where the fish had been caught that morning. For Alejandro Castillo, Father Juan Marquez had become a kind of voice narrating parts of his life. For him, the good Father had become background noise.

"How long have you been an archbishop?" asked Leenck, breaking the silence as they finished their main course. Alejandro Castillo answered and wondered why Americans were always so obsessed with occupation and the things relating to it. The dinner dragged on with none of the three exactly sure what to discuss or how to act. As dinner was being cleared, Father Juan Marquez appeared and announced the driver would be ready to take the two young men back to the Reynolds Estate after the dessert course. But then, to everyone's surprise, including likely the Archbishop himself, Alejandro Castillo announced that no, no, the young men would be staying for drinks after dessert. Father Juan Marquez could not hide the surprise on his face and simply said he would have the back terrace set up.

"Where in America are you from, Leenck?"

"Well, I have lived most of my life in California, but I was born in Spain."

"In Spain? I am originally from Spain. Where in Spain?"

"Several miles north of Barcelona."

"This is incredible. Javier, this is where our family comes from!"

Javier seemed lost in thought and, as they entered the terrace facing the garden, he simply nodded and stared blankly out at the fountains, the well-manicured strips of grass and all the intervening beds of flowers with their purples, the occasional reds and whites, the garden mirroring the colored vestments the priests wore throughout the year.

"But your name? It is not a Spanish name."

"No, my family lived deep in the woods and not in the town. I am not sure exactly where the people of my family originated, but they had been separatists and rejected the Spanish culture and language. Honestly, I think many today would call them a cult."

"Do you visit them?" The Archbishop was animated in a way he had not been in over a decade. This young man who was dying was like a strange window into his own past. And as he looked at him more closely, he began to feel an uncomfortable sensation in his chest. His heart seemed not to beat in its usual tick-tock-of-a-metronome way it always had. Instead, it seemed to be fluttering, lurching in a rhythm he had not experienced previously.

"No. I never visit them. I had a falling out with my family when I was a young man. I left. I moved to Barcelona. I learned Spanish and English. I got a job with a financial firm and learned the trade. Within a few years I moved to New York and then to California. I have never been back to Spain."

"I came here from Spain as a young priest just promoted. I haven't been back except once about ten years ago."

"And your brother? Is he in Spain?"

"My brother?"

"You know, my father . . ." Javier interjected before lifting a glass of port to his lips.

"Oh, sorry. Yes, my brother. He passed away many years ago."

"So, is Javier the only relative you see?"

"Yes, I suppose that is true." Mimicking Javier Castillo, he said: "Javier is now my only living relative."

As Alejandro Castillo said this, he noticed what I would later notice, that in profile his son looked very much like Leenck who was also, in that moment, in profile as both of them were watching a pigeon strutting along the edge of the fountain. It was as if the two profiles had been cut from the same stone by the same sculptor. Javier was darker in complexion. The two men's noses were different, the foreheads were different, but the jawline, the ears, everything else seemed similar, especially the mouths. But Alejandro Castillo didn't fully think on this the way I have. He didn't wonder why his son would look so much like this dying man who had come to the island. It was just a passing thing noticed and then passed over, left to lie unquestioned.

"Oh, this is such a funny thing, you coming from that part of Spain. Well, in some way you are like a brother then, a cousin." Alejandro Castillo probably could not believe that such words had come out of his mouth. He was not the kind of man to say such things. Clearly the surprise and excitement of this man hailing from the same part of the world from which he had come had gotten to him, affected him more deeply than he could explain. Alejandro Castillo never thought of himself as homesick much less a man buoyed by nostalgia. "I have some brandy I save for special occasions; we should all have some."

The Archbishop rang his silver bell and Father Juan Marquez ushered them all to the library where the three men then sat facing each other in a small triangle of leather armchairs. Father Juan Marquez had opened the room twenty minutes earlier and turned on the ceiling fan, had the fourth armchair removed and the remaining three positioned accordingly, placed small tables on the right side of each chair to accommodate their glasses, and set the brandy on the side table by the mantle along with three brandy snifters. He had done this just in case. As the three men sat down, Alejandro Castillo again studied the faces of his son and Leenck. There in front of him, it was then difficult to ignore that the two men really did have the same shape to their eyes, the same shape to their faces. They had the same hairline and they definitely had the same mouth. Both of them had mouths that looked a great deal the way his own mouth looked each morning in the bathroom mirror as he shaved.

"How much do you remember of Spain? Javier told me you came here to see Cassandra."

"Well, a friend brought me here to see her, but we had a falling-out and I haven't even seen him the entire week I have been here. He may have gone back to the U.S. by now."

"Well, you don't look sick like the people who come here to see Cassandra." The Archbishop continued to use the present tense the way so many do when referring to someone who had recently died.

"I'm actually very sick. I just don't look it right now. Leukemia. I have good days and bad days."

"Well, we must get together again before you leave the island." Again, such a statement from Alejandro Castillo was surprising considering what I know of him, but one must accept a story the way it is told without too many questions. The surprise that is inevitable usually justifies such inconsistencies. But as Alejandro Castillo sat there talking to Javier and

Leenck, he picked up a pen and began his nervous tic of flipping it over and over in his fingers, the pen rotating in a counterclockwise circle over and over vertically in his left hand.

"That is funny," Leenck said. "I have that bad habit too." As he said this, he pulled a small wooden triangle from his pocket and began doing the same motion with his fingers, flipping and flipping the item over and over with his left hand.

"What is that?" asked the Archbishop as he put the pen down next to his drink on the small side table. As he said this, Javier Castillo rose and excused himself to the terrace to smoke. This went almost unnoticed by the Archbishop, who was at that point utterly transfixed by Leenck and the way he flipped the wooden triangle over and over in his left hand.

"Not sure what it is exactly. A wooden coin?"

"Where did you get it?"

"My father. Apparently, the men in my family are all woodworkers, carpenters. I think they have been woodworkers for centuries. My father told me a long time ago that every boy born into our family gets one made for him. It is the only thing I have kept from my time growing up in Spain. I guess I brought it with me because, well, I doubt I will make it back to California . . ."

"Let me see it. May I? See it?"

Alejandro Castillo took the small thing Leenck had been turning over and over in his hand. Wooden. Triangular in shape. Polished smooth. And there in the center was the same small axe he had studied patiently and repeatedly for years on his own triangular wooden coin. He looked again at Leenck and saw again many of the features he could see on Javier's face, on his own face. He turned the wooden amulet over and over in his left hand instinctively. In that moment, Alejandro Castillo was lost in his own head, that forest in his dreams suddenly present and dark yet vivid in detail. And for a brief moment, he believed he could smell the forest he had not set foot in for a lifetime. Can you blame a man for such ridiculous things when placed in such a circumstance?

"You do that as if you have held such a strangely-shaped thing in your hands before," Leenck said. Alejandro Castillo did not respond. He could not respond. He handed the small wooden triangle back to Leenck and excused himself. Within a minute, Father Juan Marquez appeared and announced the driver was ready. He explained the Archbishop was not feeling well. He then fetched Javier Castillo from the terrace and ushered both of them outside to the car. As the car made its way back down the long and winding driveway to the main road by the sea, Alejandro Castillo watched the red tail lights navigate the almost-darkness of evening transitioning to night. He turned to look at the small ornamental box he kept on his chest of drawers. He could hear Father Juan Marquez call out to him to check if he was okay, and he responded that he was fine but tired, that he had maybe had too much to drink. Alejandro Castillo stared at the small ornamental box in which he kept his own wooden triangle. He would never again open that box. He would never again hold that small wooden triangle almost exactly like the one I found years later, the one I know belonged to Leenck and which I have kept all these years.

X. Practice

No one likes to admit it, but preparing for death takes practice. For some, it takes many years of practice, though I know for some it is a much easier feat. Javier Castillo spent the majority of his life ignorant of death but, in the short span of six months, his mother, his aunt, and then his father passed away. And then, the one man he had taken pity on, taken into his home, the one who had traveled to the island as his final act, the one who arrived as his own mother had died, was dying. It was not as if Javier Castillo had not anticipated this young man dying. From the first day he met him, the man Leenck had been dying, made it a point of reminding him almost daily. He reminded everyone. But despite all of the recent practice he had with death and dying, Javier Castillo felt the strange need to do something now that a man was dying in front of him in his own house. He set out on that otherwise very dull Saturday morning for the Farmer's Market. He set out to find Sister Juan Martín because he knew that week after week she would be there making her rounds around 9:30 a.m.

Javier did not use the driver that morning, nor did he take the car himself. He was always very specific about this when he recounted the events of that day. He chose to walk. He chose, instead of driving, to make the thirty-five-minute walk: down the steps of the Great House, down the sinuous driveway, down past the stunted flamboyant tree standing near the gate holding its branches covered with red petals out over the road, down the road that followed the shore around the island. Like the majority of people, he walked in the dirt alongside the edge of the road because there was no sidewalk, the sea to his right and the sound of waves crashing along the cliff side below him. Like his mother, like the Reynolds family before her, everyone in Port Town knew Javier Castillo. I guess it is safer to say that everyone knew who he was. And as he walked, the old women on the side of the road drinking their coffee or talking in hushed voices lowered their heads and offered up a respectful "Morning, Sir." Despite the fact they knew Javier Castillo was of Latin blood like many of them were, the son of Cassandra Diaz, even *el pueblo* offered up their salutations in English out of what some would assume to be respect for the man who lived in the Great House on the Reynolds Estate. English, they used English, something that does not go unnoticed for many like me. They used a language that, for many of us, is even more tainted than the Spanish we inherited.

As Javier Castillo passed the Archbishop's mansion, he kept an eye on the far-right window on the second floor. It wasn't so much that he expected the shadow of his father the Archbishop to be found there. He looked up simply to check the window of his father's room. In his mind, he was simply paying "respects" to the man others believed was his uncle, the man people had feared in ways quite different from the way they had feared his mother. As he followed the winding road, he stopped and looked back at the mansion. He felt quite sure he was being watched and, as he thought about this, he knew that in one of the windows up there Father Juan Marquez was surely watching him. As this thought registered, a young man came running through the gates to the mansion calling out "Señor Castillo, Señor Castillo." The errand boy Javier had seen many times at the Mansion had been sent to check and make sure everything was okay, to tell him that a driver from the Archbishop's Mansion could take him where he needed to go if his own car was unavailable. But Javier Castillo simply corrected the boy, told him everything was okay, told him that he simply desired a walk that morning.

Within ten minutes, the Archbishop's Mansion was far behind Javier Castillo, still visible up on the hill, but far enough away that he knew Father Juan Marquez was no longer watching him. And farther back, in the distance, farther up at the base of Mutton Hill, he could see the Great House perched there looking out over the town and the harbor. As he began the slow slope down to the marketplace near the docks, Javier Castillo would certainly have seen the people bustling near the stalls. The sea in the harbor glimmered and flickered its reflections of the morning sunlight that day much as it had centuries earlier, much as it still does today, the mountainsides remaining in shadow. He had been born on this island, but the sight of the harbor still surprised him at times. It continues to surprise me even today. Right there before him, this very sight that so easily convinced the Spaniards and then the English that this place must have been filled with gold, with gems, the way it shimmered and reflected light the way those very things they loved did; I cannot say with any certainty what it convinces anyone of today.

At the end of the main pass through the market, Javier Castillo could see Sister Juan Martín, the old Reverend Mother. She would slowly make her way through the market, as she always did, stopping to check with each stall's occupants. The nuns ran the market, but everyone who had an ounce of sense in their heads knew this was the way the Sister kept an eye on everyone and what they were doing. Sister Juan Martín was a Reverend Mother, but no one called her anything but Sister. And she never asked for anything more, never asked to be called Mother, not even by the other nuns in the convent. As Javier Castillo made his way through the people, the respectful greetings they offered him were so commonplace he barely heard them. He had watched his mother when he was a young man and how she made her way through crowds of people on the rare occasion she left the Great House. Like her, he said nothing in response to these greetings but simply watched as they stopped whatever they were doing to move out of his way. Surely the ones offering greetings would have fallen over dead had Javier Castillo responded. It would have made no difference what language he had spoken, English, Spanish, gibberish. The mere act of response would have been a truly memorable thing for them, one they would likely recount for a long time to come. As he made a beeline for the old nun, she noticed him and paused to wait for him.

"Javier? Is Teresita okay? Señora Grise?"

"They are fine, Sister. They are both well."

"Then why are you here at the market? I assumed one of them must be sick for you to come here."

"They are at the house, Sister. I asked them to come another day. I came specifically to talk to you."

"To me? Whatever can I do for you, Javier?" As with many things Sister Juan Martín said, this was not really a question.

"Is there somewhere we can sit and speak privately for a minute or two?"

"Is this about your uncle? I know that his passing had to be difficult for you. It was difficult for all of us."

"No, Sister. This is about a different matter."

Sister Juan Martín asked Javier to wait for her by the patio outside the small restaurant near the end of the market, explained that she would only be another ten minutes. Javier Castillo complied without hesitation. He sat and listened to the fisherman haggle with the restaurant owner, a daily occurrence despite the fact the restaurant owner always won the battle of pricing. Sitting there quietly awaiting the Reverend Mother, Javier was like almost every other person that lived here. He would not be treated with even an ounce of preference by any of those nuns. They were, for lack of a better word, impartial. The sisters were never disrespected, much less disregarded. They were never ignored. And as she had promised, she found him at the patio exactly ten minutes later. "Javier, would you mind returning with me to the convent?" As usual, this was not a question. Even then, the old nun's words carried a weight most of us could never explain. Her words entered the air with a decisive quality one would only expect from a noble woman in the Spanish Court, in the royal courts now found only in history books or period movies.

As Javier entered the grounds of the tiny convent, as he looked around at the well-tempered gardens, many memories came back to him. It was there he remembered as a child going to visit his mother. He remembered the plum trees there and how in early spring the branches erupted in petals, the entire convent surrounded by the pinkish haze of them. What Javier Castillo did not remember, could not remember, was that he had been born in that very convent, born in a small cell of a room in which his mother had been locked away. And there, in the yard, the shak shak tree under which his grandmother one dark night had told him to concentrate on his mother inside the walls of the convent.

The shak shak tree, the flamboyant tree, the one named the royal poinciana by the English, was brought to the island by the Spaniards. To be honest, they likely brought it inadvertently, brought it like they did their language, to the Canary Islands, Hong Kong, Florida, southwestern Texas and even the Rio Grande Valley in Arizona. But let us be honest here, the Spaniards did very few things inadvertently. About the only thing they brought inadvertently was disease. Like the Spanish language itself, the shak shak tree could be found wherever the Spaniards had been, even in the Pacific. Even its seeds perpetuated the idea of Spain as they were used inside maracas.

Javier had forgotten this, all of this. He was amazed that he had somehow forgotten this. He had forgotten his grandmother under that tree and her deep set eyes as she told him to concentrate on his mother, had forgotten the way she had placed both of her hands on his shoulders to calm him. She slowly told him over and over to concentrate on his mother inside the convent and the surprise when, minutes later, he found himself in his mother's locked room standing in front of her, the tears running down her face as she marveled at the act he had just performed. The shak shak tree in front of him, covered in the blood-red petals like the one at the gate to the Reynolds Estate, had recovered this distant memory, one he couldn't believe he had forgotten. It was the memory of the very first time he had "bent light" as his mother and his Tía Flora had called it.

Why had he forgotten this? As he walked with Sister Juan Martín through the gardens toward the main building, Javier Castillo felt a desperation in his chest as he wondered what else he had forgotten, what else he had buried deeply and successfully within his own head. Instructed by his grandmother, yes. And yet he had forgotten, had spent his life believing that the first time he had performed this act of disappearing was years later in his childhood. But at five years old, he had already discovered what even to his final day he had called his "affliction." And again, the image of his grandmother came to him, a woman about whom he knew so little. She had been there with him in the gardens of the convent, had somehow coached him to perform his first unnatural act.

As they entered the main building of the convent, Sister Juan Martín directed him to a small parlor off the main entryway and motioned him to sit by a small desk. The nun took her place behind the desk and suddenly looked quite officious to Javier. With not a single word, she gathered up some loose papers on the desk, opened one of the desk drawers, and placed them inside it with the speed and ease of a long-standing bureaucrat.

"Sister. A young man has been living at my house . . ."

"Yes, the American with cancer."

"Yes, Sister. In the last two days, he has become feverish and no longer makes sense when he speaks."

"Have you contacted the doctor?"

"No, Sister, the young man asked me not to do that months ago when he arrived. And I am sure you know I would never contact that doctor. But the young man says he is not curable and did not want to prolong the whole thing anyway."

"But he came here to see your mother, did he not? People only came to this island to see your mother because they wanted to be cured of illness."

"Well, this brings me to why I am here, Sister. Leenck, the young man, says he came here not really to see my mother but because he wanted to appease a friend and because he didn't want to die in the United States."

"I am not understanding you, Javier."

"I can speak in Spanish if you like, Sister."

"No, no. I understand the words you use, but I don't understand what it is I can do for you." As she said this, she picked up a pencil and placed it in a small box at the side of her desk. When Javier recounted this not long after the whole thing happened, he spared not even a single detail. I believe he even remembered the pencil appeared as if it had just, moments before, been sharpened.

"I think Leenck wants to make amends with this friend of his before he dies, but I don't know who he is."

"But Javier, isn't it best to ask this young man where to find his friend?"

"He doesn't know where his friend is. And I don't know the friend, even though he is from the island and not a tourist. And, as I mentioned, he is no longer making much sense when he speaks."

"And you assume I know who this friend is and even where he can be found?"

"Yes, Sister. And I hoped as a favor to my mother that you would help me."

"Javier, I will help you because you ask for help, and not because of any favors owed to Cassandra."

Javier Castillo had not heard his mother's formal name in many years. It unsettled him. When people spoke of his mother, she was always "Cassie." Sister Juan Martín picked up a book from the desk, turned slightly, and reached behind her to place it on the bookshelf. She displayed no emotion that Javier could verify. He always described the old nun to me as a warm stone, though I have never encountered anything like warmth from her over the many years. As she turned back from the bookshelf to the desk, as she looked then directly into his face, she said: "Javier, you do not look well. Have you been sick?" Javier Castillo made some remarks about being tired, about the work of keeping the Estate running, the distillery etc. To this, the nun said nothing in response. She waited a minute as if deciding whether or not to speak. "Diego Flores, Gran Señor Flores's only son. I am sure you could ask his sister about his whereabouts."

"Teresita has a brother?"

"Yes, Javier. Her brother is the man you want to find. Diego Flores brought the young man staying at your house to the island."

On the walk back to the Great House, Javier Castillo felt both confused and the very real desire to laugh out loud. This is not dissimilar to the way I felt when I first heard all of this. The woman who took care of his house, had taken care of the house for his mother in her last years, Teresita Flores, was in fact my sister, the sister of the very man he needed to find. One part of him seemed surprised by this information, but another part of him thought only of the "threads" his Tía Flora had always talked about, the fact that there are threads between everyone, even when you cannot see them. The island was small, but it wasn't small enough for this to feel like anything but the oddest of coincidences to Javier. Other people might have been disturbed by this coincidence, but not Javier Castillo. If anything, it now proved to him that he was meant to take in Leenck, the man then dying at the Great House. Diego Flores. He then felt certain he was meant to meet me, this man named Diego Flores. Javier Castillo had no idea then why he was meant to meet me, but he knew that throughout his life nothing had ever happened by coincidence, purely by coincidence.

As Javier Castillo walked back up the drive and approached the Great House, he called out to his driver to fetch the car and be ready to take Teresita into town. As Javier neared the steps to the House, the front door opened and Teresita bowed her head while asking him when he would like to have his lunch. Javier Castillo asked about Leenck and then told Teresita to go into town and bring her brother back to the House. Teresita did not look at Javier Castillo. She did not question. She had never questioned Javier Castillo or his mother in the years she worked at the Great House. She merely nodded. Javier Castillo told her the driver was waiting for her at the car and would drive her into town to get her brother. He then stepped inside, crossed the living room to the back hallway, and made his way down to the small bedroom that had once been a servant's room many years ago before his mother had inherited the House, back when she was younger and had declared no servants were to live inside the House. Leenck had been staying there as he had become too weak to climb the long staircase to one of the bedrooms on the upper floor. When Javier told the story, he was always very careful to state that when he entered the room he noted the stillness of it. There was a quiet in the room, everything motionless and calm. Within seconds, he realized Leenck was not just lying there asleep but dead. I am fairly sure that when he first told me this he did so purely to gauge my response.

First his mother, then his aunt, and then his father, the Archbishop. But then, there, lying in front of him, another person dead. Javier Castillo knew it then without a doubt that he was studying death, that he was somehow being made to study death after the rapid succession of events over the prior six months. As he stood there, he noticed what his father had noticed, what I have noticed, that Leenck looked a great deal like him, that many of his features were the same ones he had seen in the mirror. And Javier was disturbed by this resemblance. When he first recounted this to me, this is the part that bothered him the most. He wondered if his mind were playing tricks on him, if this were not, in fact, a message from the other world. But it wasn't a message from the afterlife. Leenck did look a lot like Javier. I noticed this the minute I met Javier. The plain truth of it was that Leenck and Javier were cousins; their fathers, brothers. The Archbishop was none other than the youngest brother of Leenck's father, the brother who had gone missing in the Dark Forest as a small child.

Javier Castillo left the room and went to sit in his sunroom. He drank coffee and, for the first time in weeks, smoked a cigarette. He sat silently and read the newspaper, trying as best as he could to emulate a typical late morning in his life living at the Great House. Maybe a half hour later, he heard the gravel beneath the tires crunching and crackling as the car came up the drive. A few minutes passed before Teresita motioned me into the sunroom. Javier Castillo gestured to us with his right hand.

"Señor," I said, "my sister said you requested me, but I don't . . ."

"Your friend Leenck is dead."

"He is dead?"

"Yes, Señor Flores, dead."

The directness with which Javier Castillo announced this surprised me. It likely made him, for the first time in his adult life, realize he was much more like his father, the Archbishop, than he had ever wanted to admit. As Javier looked up, he could see the tears uncontrollably running down my face. Javier Castillo did not expect this and, without thinking, rose from his chair and offered me his handkerchief. As he did so, I began to openly sob. I cannot remember a time in my life before where I felt so completely betrayed by my own body.

"I wanted him to come see Cassie," I said. "I wanted him to be okay." The words came out garbled and strange as the sobs stuttered my voice and breath.

"Unfortunately, my mother was already dead when he arrived here."

"If he had only listened. I tried to . . . If he . . ."

"She was already dead the morning that you arrived on the island. She was dead by the time your boat docked."

Teresita brought a cool wet towel to me to wipe my face. She looked confused but also concerned for her only brother. Javier Castillo stood there watching the two of us. It is difficult for me to remember exactly what happened at this point, but I believe I asked Teresita to let me sit somewhere for a minute, and she took me to one of the sitting rooms off the main entry. But Javier Castillo followed and sat in an armchair across from me.

"I wish I had known you were on the island. I would have sent for you earlier."

"So, you're a Diaz. You are Cassie's son?" I needed to change the subject, needed to pull myself together.

"I am Cassie's son, but I am a Castillo, not a Diaz. I'm sorry I haven't introduced myself. I'm Javier Castillo."

"Diego Flores, though I guess you already know that."

I couldn't help staring at Javier Castillo. I couldn't help but remember how years before, while traveling for work, I had picked up a grifter outside Los Angeles, a man who stayed with me for almost three months and then disappeared. That man spoke often of a Javier Castillo, a man who could vanish into thin air. And I knew then, as certainly as I know anything, that right then and there as I stared openly at Javier Castillo, he was this very man. The Javier Castillo in front of me with this common name had to be, nonetheless, the very same man, the same man I worried would appear in a chair in my bedroom those many years before. Of course you know he was the same man. Why else would I be telling you any of this? Of course we all know that this was the very same Javier Castillo. Another coincidence? Of course not. I wanted to laugh then, but the grief of Leenck's death confused me, confused almost every emotion I had within me.

"I wanted to head back to the U.S. I wanted to leave him here, but I couldn't. I just couldn't get myself . . ."

"Was he your lover?" Javier Castillo asked me, again with the directness of the Archbishop.

"No! He was a friend, a good friend. Nothing more. We had been neighbors in Santa Monica."

"I am sorry. I wasn't thinking. I just . . ."

"We were just friends. Nothing more, man. He was just a close friend."

"Well, I am sorry about his passing."

"I just didn't expect it to happen like this. You know it is going to happen, but you don't ever really expect it, or know exactly when it will happen."

"Well, there is no one way, my friend." As the words left his mouth, I wondered why Javier Castillo had called me, a man he didn't even know, his friend. This was followed by the even more surprising: "Please stay the afternoon."

Javier Castillo telephoned Father Juan Marquez at the Archbishop's Mansion, and the priest assured him he would take care of everything. Men came within the hour and removed Leenck's body. The funeral took place three days later. It was a small gathering with Father Juan Marquez saying the mass. For reasons none of us completely understood, Father Juan Marquez said the mass in Spanish. He must have recalled Leenck had been born in Spain, not far from his former boss. Or maybe he did it for Javier or for me. I am not sure. Neither of us would have cared if he had done the mass in English. He could have said the mass in Latin and none of us would have cared. Teresita insisted he said the mass in Spanish out of respect, a claim I can neither confirm nor deny. My sister and I were there at Santa Maria Estrella del Mar for the mass and the entire service, but I shed no tears that hot afternoon. When we all returned to the Great House, Teresita asked to go home to check on our father. Javier Castillo told her she could just return the following day as he didn't need her and knew our Father was old and unwell. As she left the house, Javier went to the bar in the library, took a bottle of rum from one of the cabinets and came to join me on the back terrace, a space he apparently almost never visited, preferring instead to sit in the sunroom looking out at the gardens. From the terrace, the insistent sounds of the sea crashing against the cliff side well below the house could be heard and little else.

"Whispers. You hear that? The ocean sounds like whispers." I said.

"Many things other than the ocean whisper, Diego. This land is haunted, you know. It may well be my dead grandfathers and grandmothers whispering."

I wasn't listening very closely to Javier Castillo. I wish I had been. I have replayed that moment in my head many times looking for clues but have found none, not a single one. I know he said more, something about the whispers, but I assumed then that whatever he said was somehow to poke fun at the flowery language I had just used about the ocean whispering.

"You can stay here, Diego. You don't have to stay with your father."

"I don't know what to say to that. I'm not sure what the hell I'm going to do."

"No, seriously, you can stay here. I know from talking to Teresita that you and your father don't speak much."

"This is true. We haven't been on good terms for a very long time." In that moment, I felt so incredibly tired. This was my life? This was in no way the life I had imagined even a year before. I was back where I had started, back on that godforsaken island that people foolishly fought over centuries ago with the belief there was gold and wealth here. But honestly, this was not remotely where I believed I would be. And who on earth would fight over this rock sitting in a blue-green sea now?

"Better then to stay here. It isn't like there isn't enough space, right?" Javier poured two glasses of rum, filled them almost to their tops, so much so that as he brought them over rum spilled over the sides of each of them.

"I want to go back to Santa Monica, but I just don't belong there. As silly as it sounds, I don't know where I belong."

"Men like us don't really belong anywhere."

I did not question Javier's statement then or the way he emphasized the word "belong" as he said what he said. I sat and sipped the rum. We both sipped rum until we were laughing and telling dirty jokes about the people in the town. Within an hour, the bottle of rum was empty, and the two of us were friends in a way only grief and alcohol can cement.

"I'm sorry I didn't come looking for you sooner. I regret that now. I am pretty sure Leenck wanted to make amends with you."

"Well, things happen . . ." As I said this, we both began to laugh, the rum now settling in to our systems.

"Yes, you are right. Things happen."

"Man, why is it so goddamned hot here?"

"Well it is summer!" The two of us laughed some more and I opened my shirt, my skin shining with perspiration.

"Oh, what the hell." As Javier Castillo said this, he took off his shirt altogether, his brown skin, like mine, damp with sweat.

Laughing, I removed my shirt as well. "This is like strip poker without cards," I said. But I went a step further and took off my pants, the two of us laughing the entire time.

"Without cards!" Javier stood and took off his pants as well, the two of us now standing there in our underwear.

The two of us stood on the terrace drinking rum and laughing. The Great House was empty except for the two of us and our intermittent laughter: more jokes, more discussion of growing up in that place and the fact neither of us knew the other until then. It is funny how clearly one can remember moments like this. As we continued joking and laughing, Javier Castillo took off his boxer shorts and stood facing the sea off to the side of the house, the sunlight flush against him.

"You said men like us don't belong anywhere. What kind of man do you think I am?" As I said this to him, I, too, removed my underwear. I laughed and stumbled as I was removing my left leg from the briefs. I barely caught myself on the edge of one of the tables before falling. And slowly, very slowly, I realized that Javier Castillo had helped to catch me and was holding my arm. "You are a man like me." As Javier Castillo said this, he bent and kissed my forearm while fixing his eyes on me to register my response. "Just like me," he repeated with exactly equal emphasis on each of the three words.

*

Months after Leenck's funeral and that drunken afternoon, I hitched my horse at the edge of the yard. I had ridden out to the edge of the property beyond the hill and surveyed the eastern orchards. The property was larger than I had guessed as a child staring up at the Great House from the harbor. As I walked toward the Great House, I could see that Señora Grise was waiting for me on the back terrace.

"Señor Flores, Señor Castillo asked that when you came back from your ride that you review some papers he left on his desk for you in his study."

"Thank you, Señora Grise. I'll take a look at them after lunch. I'm starving."

"Teresita has your lunch already prepared for you, Señor."

As I ate my lunch that afternoon, I looked out at the gardens and beyond them to the cane fields and orchards that could be seen from this side of the hill. I couldn't believe it, couldn't help but wonder how any of this had happened. I was the land agent of the Estate, the Reynolds Estate, the very one I had looked up at from the town my entire childhood. Javier Castillo had not only asked me to live there at the Great House but had turned over the entire operation of the Estate to me. Part of me would never get used to that. Part of me would always be that poor boy who lived in a two-room house with his parents and sister. As I stared out the window, I caught my reflection in the glass. My eyes were a deeper shade of brown than I had remembered, dark and deep. The image of myself, poor as it was in the window, startled me.

Memories, like ghosts, were indeed everywhere on that land. And the cats, the ones everyone in the town used to eye with suspicion, the ones that had belonged to Javier's mother, now feral, were rarely sighted on the land anymore. They had long since stopped trying to re-enter the House. I felt I had everything, which should have been a warning right then and there. I felt I had everything, even a man who gave himself over to me completely. As I sat there eating lunch and thinking about all of this, I remembered the papers Señora Grise had mentioned, and I got up quickly and went to Javier's study to review them.

The papers on the desk, lying in a neat stack, were legal documents.

As I reviewed them, I realized it was Javier's will. As I read and read, it became clear that Javier Castillo had designated the house, the land, the rum distillery, all of it to me should he die. There were so many pages of the document I couldn't read it carefully. I scanned through them, enough to register the request that ten percent of the estate's earnings should go to James Reynolds, the Governor General, or his heirs, in perpetuity. I leafed through the stack of papers and then returned them to the neatly set way I found them. I wanted them, for some reason, to be as if I had never touched them. When I returned to the sunroom, I found Javier Castillo sitting there, reading the newspaper.

"Javi, I didn't hear you come in."

"Have you reviewed the papers?"

"I have, but . . ."

"I wanted you to know about them in case when I am gone there is any trouble with the Governor General."

"But why now, Javi?"

"I need to be prepared, *papi*. That's all. The lawyers filed the papers this morning."

Practicing for death. I had heard these words and variations of them from Javier Castillo many times over the months I had lived at the Great House with him. With each strange story he told me, there was the sense he was practicing. I didn't understand it then. In many ways, I don't understand it now. And through the entire time I had been living there, the long-gone grifter would time and time again surface in my head. Ricardo Blanco. That was the man's name, the one who talked and talked about a man named Javier Castillo, a man who could disappear before one's very eyes. But in Javier's tales, the last name Blanco was never used. There was Ricardo and Rosa, their sons Pedro and Carlos, a host of other characters. And despite many opportunities to watch Javier Castillo, not once in those months had I seen him disappear. For a brief time then, I even began to wonder if he were in fact the same Javier Castillo I had heard about almost daily in those months I had been with the grifter.

One evening, maybe a week after the will had been signed, Javier Castillo requested a special dinner, French cuisine, something he almost never did. Señora Grise and Teresita were sent into town to request the chef at the lone four-star hotel come to the house to cook this meal, and he came without hesitation. Javier Castillo was in essence a Reynolds. He may not have been English, did not have the Reynoldses' build, but he was, to the people of the island, a Reynolds now. No one, except for me and Teresita, spoke to him in Spanish.

After the elaborate dinner that evening, after the after-dinner brandy, after the surprising announcement that he would take some rum on the back terrace with me, after the said rum was consumed, Javier Castillo retired to his room. He was tired, immensely tired. Once he had taken off his clothes and gotten into bed, once I heard the click of the light switch as he turned off the lights, I opened the door that connected my room to his and entered quietly. Without a word between us, I got into bed next to Javier Castillo as I had done night after night since I began living there.

"I am surprised you asked Marcel to come cook tonight."

"Why, *papi*? He is a good chef."

"Just surprised me, that's all."

"Well, good! I am glad I can still surprise someone."

"Did you ever know a man named Blanco?" The question slipped from my mouth and into the air of the room.

"Blanco? No. I don't remember a Blanco. Is he one of the farm-hands?"

"No, just someone I met many years ago in California. Never mind."

"Actually, I do remember a man named Blanco. Yes, from a very long time ago."

"Did you love him, Javi? Did you . . ."

"Go to sleep, *papi*. I am tired."

"But did you . . ."

"Go to sleep, Diego."

The moonlight was bright and crisp; it illuminated the sheer curtains by the window, gave them a visible life as they occasionally ballooned out due to the breeze coming in from the sea. I felt quite certain Javier was lying, that he had, in fact, loved the Blanco man, but I left the issue alone. What else could I have done then? Trust me, I have thought about this countless times since that night. Within a short time, I fell asleep. All night, I had strange dreams. In each of them, Ricardo Blanco made an appearance, his green eyes sharp and intense. What happened to Ricardo Blanco? I had gotten up one morning and the grifter was gone. No note. Nothing. He just disappeared. In one of the dreams, Ricardo was lying on the asphalt of the parking lot outside the motel where I had first met him. In another, Ricardo was trying desperately to explain the vanishing man, the man named Javier Castillo. And finally, the dream that woke me: Ricardo stabbing his hands into Javier's chest repeatedly, the hands sinking into his chest as if they were knives.

The early sunlight coming over the mountain, the light slowly invading the fields, barely brightened the room. Sitting up in bed, I turned to see that Javier's naked body was uncovered and the sheets twisted around his calves, the sheets damp with sweat. Javier Castillo's face was calm, his eyes closed, but his body seemed wrenched and in discomfort. I tried to wake him, but he only mumbled back without opening his eyes. I kept asking him if he were okay, and Javier whispered he was fine, but he did not look fine to me. He didn't look well at all. He looked sick, sickly, odd. I cannot even explain it well. Javier Castillo was covered in sweat as if he were trying to accomplish a Herculean task. The room brightened and brightened. I could hear the house coming to life, Teresita and Señora Grise downstairs about their work. And then Javier Castillo said it, said it clearly, said: "One more time, one final time."

"What are you talking about? Wake up." I said. "One final time," Javier Castillo repeated. And without fanfare, without any other warning, I noticed something incredible. I could almost make out the bed beneath Javier Castillo, the bed visible through the very shape of the man I had slept next to for months. And within another few seconds, there was a shadow, then a shimmer, and Javier Castillo was gone, only the bed and twisted sheets remaining where he had been lying. I kept calling the name "Javi" over and over, more and more urgently, but without raising my voice; I did not want to capture the attention of the staff downstairs. After five minutes, I scrambled to my feet and stared at the bed. I called out "Javi" many more times with no difference in outcome. When I realized Javier Castillo was gone, completely gone, I ran from the room and stood in my own room staring at the bed through the open door. The repetition of "Javi" became "Why did I ask him?" became "I am sorry, Javi; please come back."

Javier Castillo would never come back. Didn't we all know he would never come back? Javier Castillo had built a life around disappearing, but what was far more remarkable was the fact he could reappear somewhere else, somewhere he wanted to be. But Javier Castillo did not appear somewhere else. He did not materialize in some distant land, in a bank vault or atop a mountain. He faded away cleanly because that is how his story had to end. For a man who spent his entire life disappearing to spend the last part of his life utterly unable to do so is something you and I will never understand.

There was no fuss after his death, no visit from the old Governor General now wheelchair-bound. None of the Governor General's children or relatives demanded to see the will. There were no demands to see Javier Castillo's body. Neither my sister nor Señora Grise ever questioned my explanation that Javier had died and had requested cremation out at the edge of the orchards, that I had taken his body out there and done what I had been asked to do. Neither of them ever went out to check the site. The lawyers handled all of the transfers. The newly-made Bishop Marquez came by to offer his condolences but never so much as uttered a single question about a burial. It was as if Javier had, like his mother and aunt before him, cast an unshakeable spell over the situation. Everything simply proceeded the way Javier had requested in his papers.

Months after his death, as I went through his will with the lawyers to finalize the last step of the transfer of assets and property, there was one request buried within a paragraph I would never have noticed. Money was to be sent to a facility in Los Angeles every month for the care of one Carlos Drogón Blanco for as long as he lived. Blanco. As plain as day, in his will no less, a Blanco. Had he loved Ricardo Blanco? Or had he felt some deep guilt about the results of his actions in that one circumstance? I would never know. I did as I was told. And for over a decade I did as the will instructed until, finally, one day I received a note along with the last check I had sent, a note detailing that this younger Blanco had passed away.

Of course he was the same Javier Castillo I had heard so much about from Ricardo Blanco so many years earlier. He was the very one. A confused man wandering the streets had spoken his name out loud to me so many years ago, told me story after story of this man who could disappear. And, somehow, this very act had set in motion what I cannot help but feel was an elaborate but incomprehensible machine. Trust me, if you can, if you can trust anything I have told you, that I have thought over the entire thing so many times it would be silly to admit the exact number. Ricardo, his family, Leenck, the Diaz sisters, this island in the middle of nowhere, Spain, all of it: I have thought about it all so many times I am convinced it is what made me sick. But what can I tell you? What have I learned? I have learned that we are the Teresitas of this story, the Sister Juan Martíns, the Father Juan Marquezes. We work. We attend to the visible and certain things of this world. We try to make a life out of the solid and the fixed, even when there are flashes of a world most cannot believe exists, do not want to believe exists.

I have spent most of my adult life tending the Reynolds Estate, running the rum distillery and managing the other lands once held by this difficult family. I have spent my life recounting these stories to myself. These stories have become, more so than keeping the Estate operating, my profession. I would see Javier Castillo many times over the decades after that morning when he faded away in his bed, but in every case it was a trick of memory or, eventually, a trick of a failing mind. Every year, for thirty years, I would sit on the back terrace of the Great House on June 10th and drink rum without a speck of clothing on me. I recite parts of these stories to myself, lest even I forget them. But I won't make it to June 10th of this year. The doctors all say the same thing: I won't make it.

The Reynolds family, the Diaz family, the Castillos, and the unfortunate Blancos: do you understand now why I have had to keep recounting bits of it all? Practice, Javier would say, a kind of practice. Evening after evening now, I sit out on the terrace. And as faithfully as ever, the sea crashing below, the sea crashing against the cliff side, fills the air with whispers, the same ones I heard that afternoon so long ago. Someone else would have thought Javier Castillo himself was one of the people whispering in the air as the sun left the sky, but we know better. We have always known better.

THE END

ACKNOWLEDGMENTS

Grateful acknowledgments are made to the editors of the following journals where these stories, sometimes in slightly different versions, originally appeared:

Asian American Literary Review, Blackbird, Four Way Review, Guernica, The Hopkins Review, Normal School, and *Waxwing.*

"The Affliction" was reprinted in *The Chamber Four Fiction Anthology,* eds. Michael Beeman, Sean Clark, Eric Markowsky, Marcos Velasquez, and Nico Vreeland. (Chamber Four LLC, 2010).

As always, I would like to thank my beloved, Jacob Bertrand. I would also like to thank my family and friends for the incredible support they have given me. I specifically want to thank Christopher Castellani and Janet Silver for their encouragement and help. To my medical practice partner, Lisa Boohar, I am beyond grateful for her understanding of the time I have taken to do this work, year in and year out.

Significant gratitude is owed to the John Simon Guggenheim Memorial Foundation for a fellowship that allowed me the time to bring this collection into being. I owe a debt of gratitude to the Rockefeller Foundation for a Literary Arts Fellowship at the Villa Serbelloni/Bellagio Center, where some of the work in this collection was started. And finally, I would like to thank my editor Martha Rhodes and everyone at Four Way Books for their continued belief in my work.

Publication of this book was made possible by grants and donations. We are also grateful to those individuals who participated in our 2017 Build a Book Program:

Anonymous (6), Evan Archer, Sally Ball, Jan Bender-Zanoni, Zeke Berman, Kristina Bicher, Laurel Blossom, Carol Blum, Betsy Bonner, Mary Brancaccio, Lee Briccetti, Deirdre Brill, Anthony Cappo, Carla & Steven Carlson, Caroline Carlson, Stephanie Chang, Tina Chang, Liza Charlesworth, Maxwell Dana, Machi Davis, Marjorie Deninger, Lukas Fauset, Monica Ferrell, Emily Flitter, Jennifer Franklin, Chuck Gillett, Dorothy Goldman, Dr. Lauri Grossman, Naomi Guttman & Jonathan Mead, Steven Haas, Mary Heilner, Hermann Hesse, Deming Holleran, Nathaniel Hutner, Janet Jackson, Christopher Kempf, David Lee, Jen Levitt, Howard Levy, Owen Lewis, Paul Lisicky, Sara London & Dean Albarelli, David Long, Katie Longofono, Cynthia Lowen, Ralph & Mary Ann Lowen, Donna Masini, Louise Mathias, Catherine McArthur, Nathan McClain, Gregory McDonald, Britt Melewski, Kamilah Moon, Carolyn Murdoch, Rebecca & Daniel Okrent, Tracey Orick, Zachary Pace, Gregory Pardlo, Allyson Paty, Marcia & Chris Pelletiere, Taylor Pitts, Eileen Pollack, Barbara Preminger, Kevin Prufer, Vinode Ramgopal, Martha Rhodes, Peter & Jill Schireson, Roni & Richard Schotter, Soraya Shalforoosh, Peggy Shinner, James Snyder & Krista Fragos, Megan Staffel, Alice St. Claire-Long, Robin Taylor, Marjorie & Lew Tesser, Boris Thomas, Judith Thurman, Susan Walton, Martha Webster & Robert Fuentes, Calvin Wei, Abby Wender, Bill Wenthe, Allison Benis White, Elizabeth Whittlesey, Hao Wu, Monica Youn, and Leah Zander.